BOOKS BY C.K. SORENS

TRIMARKED SERIES

Trimarked
Afflicted
Tattered

***

THE DJINN OF LAS VEGAS

Eighteen Wishes

This novel contains content that may be triggering.
For a list of possible triggers, please visit
https://www.cksorens.com/trimarked-trigger-warnings

This is a work of fiction. All of the characters, organizations, and events portrayed in this novel are products of the author's imagination.

AFFLICTED

Edited by Travis & Whitney O. McGruder via Wit & Travesty

Cover design by www.OriginalBookCoverDesign.com

WYRDWEAVER
L L C

www.cksorens.com

ISBN 978-1-954054-11-0 (case laminate hardcover)
ISBN 978-1-954054-05-9 (jacketed hardcover)
ISBN 978-1-954054-02-8 (paperback)
ISBN 978-1-954054-03-5 (ebook)

First Edition: March 2022

To all the helpers.
Watching your bravery has helped me keep my sanity.

C.K. Sorens

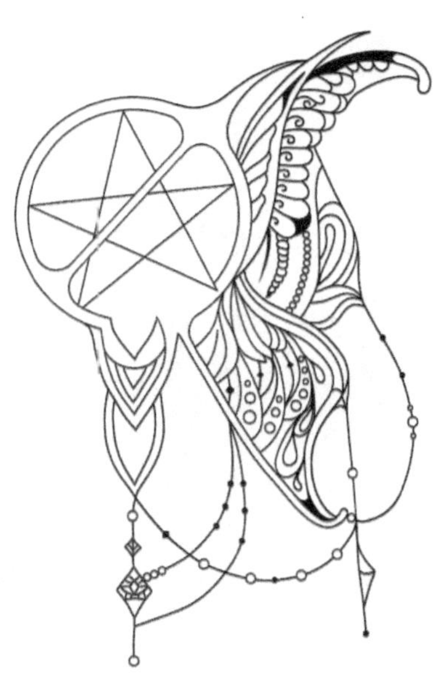

Afflicted

Trimarked Series

Book Two

1

EMBER

Fingers stabbed into Ember's hair and pulled her head back, forcing a cramp to collar around her neck.

Her heartbeat stuttered, her muscles threatened to freeze. Power buzzed within the marrow of her bones. She swallowed it all down, kept her eyes wide to see the ratty furniture that surrounded her, the peeling paint on the walls, and the bodies turning toward the commotion.

She was in a Halfer's safe house, not on her way to the End of the World. The hand in her hair did not belong to Brandt, the boy who'd hauled her across Trifecta, then threatened to kill her. He'd put her through hell, wanting her to open the domed barrier that held Trifecta and its human, Witch, and Fae residents hostage.

Brandt wasn't a threat anymore. He was locked up on Witch land somewhere, and had been for the last five weeks.

Ember half-stepped backward, spun on her heel, and smacked the restricting hand away as she came around. Another step took her inside the offending girl's guard. Ember's knee to pelvic bone attack sent a flush to pale cheeks and left the Halfer scrambling.

Because no, this wasn't Brandt, but it wasn't innocent, either. The Halfers, aware of her trauma, used small things like a tug on the long length of Ember's black hair to make her uncomfortable. Though she had randomly visited their Club for the last few years, they'd ignored her as she never held permanence. Now that she had moved in, they were not accepting.

But, like them, she had nowhere else to go. Like them, she was of mixed-blood, half human and half mage, making them unaccepted by any of the races.

Unlike them, her mother had kept her close for seventeen years. If that were their only difference, perhaps the Halfers' irritation would have faded by now, five weeks later.

While none of them fully realized what happened last month, they remembered that she brought a topside human into their ranks, uninvited. They remembered the storm that shook the mountainside with a power not seen before. They only knew the brief description Chase, their eighteen-year-old leader, provided. A human attacked her. Her mother kicked her out.

Somehow, they discovered a few details, like how Brandt had used her hair like a leash. The harassment started as mere finger brushes against the strands. She'd had the unfortunate reaction of jumping once, more against a surge of energy within her, fear of exposing herself with a few ill-timed blue sparks. They'd attributed her flinch to their actions and hadn't let up on her since.

Putting the length into a braid or bun would grant them a power over her that Ember refused to give. It would erase the 'out of sight, out of mind' phenomenon that kept her from worse treatment. Gathering her hair in any way left the Trimark tattoo visible, a clear reminder of just how different she was. Fae Binding Ink in the design of a crossed out pentacle and bordered on the right with a butterfly wing represented her curse. Its open presence would add fuel to an already white-hot fire.

For now, Ember spent minimal time with the Halfers', coming in only for meal times, like tonight's dinner. She learned to suppress the power within as it surged with their attacks. She gained more control as their efforts increased, enough so that the buzz remained low and quiet, even while Ember defended herself.

The girl, Sadie, recovered. She glared at Ember with narrowed hazel eyes, as if her greater height alone made her better than the Trimarked girl. She arched her arm toward Ember, her hips twisting with the motion to increase impact.

Ember dodged the fist aimed at her cheekbone. Sadie adjusted and thrust the power of the punch into Ember's shoulder, knocking her off balance. Teeth gritted against the pain, Ember lowered her center of gravity to get her feet back under her, then knocked her uninjured shoulder into Sadie's ribcage.

The girl stumbled backward, and an observer caught her arms to steady her. Ember didn't lose focus to check how many Halfers had found a spot at the edge of the small living room, closing her ears to threats aimed at her and encouragement meant for Sadie.

An arm wrapped around Ember's shoulders while her attention drilled into her opponent. She cursed her stupidity. Words weren't all the Halfers might throw at her. The guy behind her stood at least a head taller, was twice as wide, and thought he'd get control quickly.

They hated living with her. She got that loud and clear. But pulling hair and starting a fist fight proved poor tactics. After all, fighting was Ember's best feature.

Before his grip tightened, Ember slipped between his body and forearm. Strands of her hair floated in the friction, framing her as she focused her energy on the smaller target, eager to get Sadie out of the way first.

"Damn it, Ember," Chase shouted from the kitchen archway. The big guy grabbed Ember again and this time she looked behind. Keegan gave her a sharp shake of his head, a silent command to stop.

Chase's closest friend, Keegan, helped enforce the Halfer's rules. He loved boxing, eager to teach anyone who wanted to practice so he'd have sparring partners. After Chase caught her opening the barrier five years ago, he'd suggested Ember learn to defend herself, and sent her to Keegan. The huge Halfer hadn't been excited to gain her as a student. Still, his loyalty was to Chase first.

His place in the hierarchy convinced her he wasn't trying to fight her. She relaxed.

Stars flooded Ember's vision. She lost her breath against Keegan's hard body with Sadie's jab into her wounded shoulder. Keegan's automatic reaction was to wrap his arms around Ember to steady her. The contact sent bile into the back of Ember's throat and her skin tightened into goosebumps.

"Nice setup," Ember croaked, blinking Keegan's shocked features into focus.

"N-no. Of course that wasn't what I—"

Ember left him stumbling over his words, ignoring Chase, who stood by Sadie's side. It didn't matter if Sadie's attack had surprised Keegan, or if he'd been a part of it. Ember didn't want to give the Halfers the joy of seeing rage burning in her light grey eyes. She tucked her chin, passed by the living room's faded plaid couches and mismatched chair and got the verge out of the house.

The door she burst from was usable despite the deceivingly placed boards that stuck out around the outer sides to make the entry look nailed shut. Members of the underground were adept at creating camouflaged adjustments meant to keep them under the radar in a city that held no place for their kind.

She strode through the yard and into the street, where she stopped at its center. The Halfer zone claimed a rare stretch of neighborhood where the houses faced each other. Thick forest breaks separated the rest of the dwellings where the humans lived, all their front doors facing down the mountain instead of looking into another person's home. This reclaimed territory offered Halfers shelter with few avenues for Topsiders to sneak up on them.

If Ember had space, it was an empty street, or a quiet stretch of forest. Wherever there weren't other people.

The bright sun lowered over the trees, falling toward the valley. She closed her eyes against it, lifting her face to absorb the late autumn rays. Snow capped the mountains and would make its way to their lower slopes soon, halting most movement in Trifecta. Without gasoline available for the machines, all work had to be done by hand. The humans cleared the snow as needed. Fae and Witches walked on top of it. Ember, as heavy-footed as a human, had learned to enjoy the sunlight in these moments, to soak it in for the long haul.

A bitter bubble of sound that might be mistaken for a laugh burst softly in her throat. The long haul was all she knew in this town.

The only thing human and mage Trifectans agreed on was hating the Trimarked Child. Though they remained segregated for the most part, each race to their own piece of land, they were connected by their fear of magic. The humans feared it all. The Fae and Witches dreaded whatever Ember might become.

The circumstances of her birth were forbidden. She'd been saturated with three different forms of magic while surrounded by the power of the Veil. No one had accomplished the feat before, or dared attempt it. Until Ember's fading Wizard father tricked her mother into his scheme, resulting in Ember being bound by Fae magic and ostracized from all societies while only hours old. He'd disappeared from Trifecta, and Ember had not laid eyes on him once.

Her status was why these fights with the Halfers were

dangerous, why she'd tolerated their nasty side looks and curled lips for the past five weeks.

She had nowhere else to go.

Ember wrapped her arms around the ache in her stomach and looked skyward. Cold air filled her lungs. Fingers sunk into the plush sleeves of the black coat Chase gave her. She'd kept it on while eating, not intending to be inside for long, trying to avoid exactly what had happened.

Food and sleep were the only reasons she came by the abandoned houses situated between the human neighborhood and the Witches' Circle. Otherwise, she stayed outdoors. It wasn't new. When she'd lived with her mom, she had often wandered the parts of the forest no one went, stopping by to check on her mom and pass out for a few hours.

She thought she'd been trapped then, mandated to self-segregation. Her assigned Fae guardian, Nicu, enforced these rules. She hated to admit he'd been right.

She'd lost anonymity when her power sparked from her fingertips, ignoring the purpose of the Fae's Binding Ink. Her mom wouldn't let Ember come home when she couldn't stay away from magic.

But, hey. She owned a pretty coat. It was probably even Witch-made. New, rather than some human's hand-me-down.

There was no reason her spirit should sink along with the late autumn temperature. She had no evidence Nicu's five week silence was because he and the Fae were planning what to do with her now that they knew their Binding wasn't blocking her power. It might be taking so long because they needed to build a special cage to contain her.

Ember's lids squeezed shut, and she struggled to breathe through her pinched nose.

The front door of the house she'd escaped thrust open. Ember startled, then cursed. She refused to show the Halfers any sign of weakness, to let them think her fear of being captured had anything to do with their bullying. She risked a glance toward the house.

Chase jumped over the three steps of the front porch, his charcoal wool coat as narrow and elongated as he was with the bottom buttons undone to give his lanky legs space to move. The bag slung over one shoulder signaled it was time for her to work. Their weekly delivery of food was due to his friends on the outside of the barrier, and only she could poke a temporary hole through the otherwise impenetrable energy.

"Story is you started the fight," Chase said on his approach.

There was no point. Ember pursed her lips and stomped up the road, leaving him to catch her. She wouldn't refuse to help, no matter how he pissed her off. She owed him for clothes, and her spot under a roof, and the food that settled into a wet lump within her stomach.

With Nicu gone, the threat of the Fae sat heavy in her mind. She owed Chase a lot. She might not have a lot of time to repay him, and she needed him to owe her if she hoped to have him take care of Susan if the Fae came for Ember.

It sucked.

"I haven't gotten to where I am by believing in fairy tales," Chase continued once he reached her side. "And Keegan fessed up."

"He was in on it." Her lips thinned with the confirmation.

"Not exactly. But he didn't stop it in time, thought it would figure itself out. So now, he's doing something for you."

"Another favor," she snapped.

The ends of Chase's shaggy hair shook in denial. "He owes you. It's his job to keep the peace and he let you be egged on for weeks."

Ember curled her lips between her teeth. How long had Keegan known she'd been targeted? Had Chase?

A shudder ran from Ember's nape to the base of her spine and she stopped her thoughts hard. It sounded as if part of her expected their help, that she was surprised it hadn't come earlier. Hope was dangerous for the Trimarked girl.

The two skirted the eastern edge of the human neighborhood, which was marked by tall privacy fences on their right. Redwood pines pressed in from the left. The land cleared and displayed the Witches' immaculate fields, planted in the floodplain of the Pine River.

After a few miles of skirting the line between human and Witch property, the human neighborhood gave way to the school yard. Beyond the soccer pitches, they scaled a chicken-wire fence. Ember's shoulder twinged as she climbed, the familiar stiffness of an oncoming bruise, probably the size of Sadie's fist.

Just breathe through it. No use in dragging the girl through Trifecta to throw her out. Expulsion backfired with Brandt, after all.

The creak of pieced together windmills accompanied them to the bank of the river. Ember stopped wondering years ago when their awkward frames would fall apart. The humans were careful to keep their sources of electricity running, constantly checking and making adjustments to their designs, supported by the Witches' trade of machine parts salvaged from the industrial park they called home.

Ember and Chase reached the washed out bank, then they scrambled toward the water. More evidence of the human's scrap metal ingenuity broke the surface of the river. Hydro turbines lined the length of a small step-down waterfall, the uneven tops creating an accidental bridge. On the opposite bank, exposed tree roots of ancient redwoods worked as a natural ladder to climb up the steep side.

On solid ground, Ember took the lead. Though Chase knew the approximate location of the invisible barrier, he was more likely to run into it. They could mark the border here with little risk of wind or slope to erase it, but they didn't want to bring attention to the space where Ember completed her work.

The barrier's magic buzzed before her and awoke an answering burst in her veins. Blind to the static power until it moved, she sensed its presence, like how she felt the wind, or gravity.

Her fingers trembled when she raised them to the thick, transparent energy.

A spark flew from her fingertips. Tiny ripples of concentrated power warped in a visual mark of her manipulation. Ember jumped back, swallowed a painful gulp of air.

Chase watched her with hooded eyes, kept silent out of self-preservation. If he spoke, her fear would snap into rage.

If he left her alone, she would figure out how to do this.

She owed him. They had a deal. The guys on the outside needed to eat. Something as small as a near-death experience would not stop her from fulfilling her end of the bargain.

"It's safe, little hybrid." Though Nicu spoke the words a month ago, their memory had the same effect now as they had then.

She could fading do this.

Ember raised her fingers, and they tapped against the barrier. First finger, middle finger, ring finger, and return. A steady rhythm. There was no stickiness against her touch, no attempt by the energy to rise and wrap around her skin, to pull her in.

The hole opened. She held out her hand, and Chase placed the heavy backpack into her grip. Ember tossed it through before the break in the barrier slammed closed.

But this time it didn't spring back.

Ember's eyes burned for the need to blink. Her lungs ached with paused breath. The edges of the parting shimmered a light blue. The flickering energy sank into place and invisibility, a slow blending instead of the instant seal that she'd sworn to Brandt was the only way it ever closed.

That was before the power had swallowed her whole, suspending her above ground, overloading her capacity to feel, or think, or be.

Chase thought her reaction was relief that the barrier hadn't sucked her in again, having witnessed none of the fluctuations. She tucked her trembling fingertips under her arms, kept her thoughts to herself to uphold the illusion.

Brandt had once demanded she open a door and hold it. Make it bigger so the entire town could file out and return to life on the outside. She hadn't been able to, then. She still didn't think she was capable of something that big. This change, though. Did it mean her powers were getting stronger, or was this caused by her time in the barrier?

Movement in the outer forest was Ember's sign to go. She needed to put space between herself and Chase while he had his debriefing conversation with his spies. Her slow speed guaranteed he caught up with her at the river crossing.

"Is it still bad?" he asked.

Ember clenched her fists. Of course, he thought he had the right to ask, but she didn't owe him that much.

"I'm cold," she snapped.

Chase tucked his hands into his pockets, pulled out a pair of gloves.

She picked up her pace, leaving him and his verge-cursed offering behind.

2

EMBER

Ember and Chase continued on the narrow forest trail that led them between Witch and human lands. The first stars crept in on the tail of sunset, tiny lights fighting for their place in the ombre sky. Chase pulled out a kinetic energy flashlight to light up the path that took them north, up the mountain, and to the broken road of the Halfer's zone.

"We need to talk about the fight."

Ember wished Chase would learn to appreciate silence.

"Why?"

"It can't happen again."

Ember snorted and crossed her arms over her chest despite the ache in her shoulder, a curl on her upper lip.

"Tell your people that."

"It's a bad time right now for lots of reasons," Chase explained. "It's going to snow soon. I have to get our resources in place so everyone is ready for lockdown."

"Are you implying you won't be around to babysit me?" Ember demanded, her silver eyes flashing in the moonlight.

"Not the way I consider it," he drawled, taking her outburst in stride. His composure eased the fight from Ember, giving her brain room to think. He was the only buffer she had.

"Do you need help?" The question twisted Ember's mouth in weird ways, leaving a wrinkled brow in its wake. Yet, she sincerely meant the offer. It would keep her separated from the Halfers, and she'd be able to be of real benefit to him after everything he'd done for her.

"Well, verge. She actually asks, and I have to say no." Chase's hands flew from his pockets to the length of his hair. He combed it back with his fingers, then secured it into a short ponytail with a few sharp twists.

"Don't worry about it," Ember sped through her reply.

"No, listen. It's a thing I have to do. The woman who left me in charge wants it done in a specific way."

Ember stared at Chase, her lips parted with his confession. "What does that mean?"

"There's not much I can tell." Chase spoke, his words careful. "When Halfer infants were first abandoned, there weren't older Halfers to take them. This woman saw value in life, even in unwelcome babies. She took care of us for a while. When she wanted to leave, the oldest Halfers refused the responsibility. Verge, I didn't want it, either, but she gave it to me, anyway. I was eleven when she gave me some instructions and told me to ask the older kids for help."

"So she set up the whole underground, then left you to run it?"

Chase snorted.

"Hardly. We had to do that ourselves. We started with the houses. The human runaways taught us how to fix things up. Some even snuck back to learn how to do something we needed. Then, I fell into an agreement with—"

Chase coughed mid-sentence, but didn't take up the narrative. Either he ran out of breath or he ran into words he couldn't share. Ember held her questions this time, grateful for what he offered. Not because of content, but because he'd chosen to tell her.

It reminded her of when her mother had been healthier,

and she'd read Ember to sleep. Chase had known she hadn't recovered from her scare at the barrier, and he'd told her a story. She wouldn't push him for more after that.

At the northernmost road of the human neighborhood, Ember stopped in the center of the t-junction where worlds parted. Thoughts of bedtime stories invaded her heart, and she looked along the last paved street.

"Let's check on her."

He didn't ask or offer, and that made it okay.

The pair walked close to the treeline on the south side of the street. Though a few young pines had wiggled in, the majority of the trees were maple or birch. Whoever planned the step-down roads of Trifecta had planted them after tearing the mountainside up for construction. The deciduous thickets within the evergreen forest provided a visual break between the southern facing houses, hiding humanity between the rows.

Almost as if whoever did it knew they'd want to hide.

Ember shook off the thought. Privacy was the more likely reason, or to create the illusion of living rural, rather than in a city built around the industry of making glass and bottled water.

They passed the last well-cared-for house, and black pavement transformed into sparse gravel. The slope rose sharply on their right. Halfway between the road and the elevated tree line, an old maintenance building broke the surface of the hill, grey as if it were a massive, trapezoidal boulder in the midst of dead grass.

A low flicker danced across the semi-circular window set into the top third of the door. The small box television was on, as always. At this time of day, the lone station would be static. Most likely, Susan slept.

Ember's throat tightened around the thought that she wasn't allowed inside to check.

"There isn't any smoke from the furnace," Chase mumbled.

Ember shook her head, her attention fixed on the quiet flickers through the window.

"She'll be using the oven." Chase's feet shifted on the gravel as he turned to face her. "The heater has never worked," she shrugged. His frown showed he was not satisfied with the answer.

"Fade it all, Ember, why didn't you tell me?"

"Beyond the scope of our deal."

Chase's chest expanded and gathered air for the forceful sigh her words inspired.

"You underestimate the importance of your particular skill."

"I understand the value of a kept secret," she countered.

"What about the value of a good asset?"

Ember set her lips against a reply. So she could send food out to kids who preferred to rough it outside Trifecta more than having some semblance of comfort inside. Or, better yet, move on to a city not trapped in the Veil. What could they possibly report to Chase, anyway, for it to have the benefit he claimed?

It wasn't enough, not after everything he'd done for her and Susan. It was time to be done with this.

She retraced their steps, leaving her mom alone for another night. As she scanned the area out of habit, Ember caught movement at the edge of the forest behind her mother's house. Her feet froze with the person-shaped outline of a shadow, one taller than either Branna or Nicu, her usual Fae guards.

"What is it?" Chase murmured, his body very close to hers. Ember shook her shoulders and stepped away, trying to throw off his clinging heat. Whoever it was had disappeared. If it was the Fae, at least they weren't interested in capturing her. Yet.

"Let's go."

"Remembering No Man's Land?" Chase asked.

"No, but thanks for the reminder."

Ember shuddered, the revulsion almost enough to break through the chill of having an unknown Fae so close. She had no desire to think about the place at the center of Trifecta where Brandt had stabbed Aaron before marching her to the End of the World. If anything, it was more reason to get the verge out of here.

They kept to the southside treeline on their way back. Three houses in, Ember glanced left, then at the toes of her new, hole-free shoes. She hated this street.

"You could knock on his door."

Why the fades was Chase so observant tonight?

"And out him to his dad?" Ember asked. "Tell the world the Trimarked girl wants to thank the human Golden Boy for helping get rid of his human best friend who tried to kill her?"

"Do you need a breath?" Chase's thick voice sounded suspiciously like it hid a chuckle. Ember bit her tongue inside the secrecy of her mouth.

"You've become far too accommodating." Ember slanted her eyes, the expression wasted on Chase whose face was hidden behind the hood of his coat. Was this because of the fight? Or her fear at the barrier? Did he feel bad for her?

Ember swallowed, only so she wouldn't snarl.

Back at the junction of solid pavement next to the broken road, and into the Halfer zone. Chase's flashlight brightened an otherwise treacherous walk in the dark. Ember clung to her balance, determined not to give Chase a chance to continue his odd desire to be nice by supporting her.

Chase stopped Ember from heading to the house in which she'd been sleeping. She didn't mind, not in any hurry to slip in and try to find herself an inconspicuous corner. He used his own curved path to direct her feet toward the first house on the right, a small bungalow.

Ember refused to move, not understanding the change.

"Just go." A bit of comfort filled Ember with the frustrated vibration of his voice. That was more like Chase.

Inside, Ember found a well-maintained, peaceful home. It was the opposite of the catch-all space she'd left earlier. The surfaces were clean. Though the furniture was decades old, there were no holes in the upholstery. The front was a combined living room and kitchen. A hallway leading deeper in opened at the center of the back wall.

"What's this?" Ember stopped inside the door. Chase didn't share her reluctance. He jerked out of his coat and threw it over the couch.

"It's mine," he said. "After tonight, Keegan thought you might want his room."

Or Chase had made him give it to her. Ember curled her shoulders, her fingers rested against her thighs. She kept them from tapping when she saw Chase glance at her on his way around the peninsula into the kitchen.

"That's..." Not going to go over well.

"Hey," Chase called from where he stood in the open door of his refrigerator. "What happened showed us the Halfers need a reminder of how to behave. Keegan is making the rounds to help them."

Ember blinked away a burn in her eyes and her lips thinned. Right. Everyone to their own community, with pretty much the same set of rules. Stay with your own. Stay clear of others.

Even she had the same rules. She just didn't have the neighborhood.

Safer here than with the Fae.

The coat Ember held weighed in her tired arms. The ache in her shoulder pulsed now that their hike was over. Fighting came to mind. The truth was, she wanted to give in.

"Where's the room?" Keegan's, not hers.

"Down the hall on the left. Bathroom's at the end."

A queen mattress sprawled on a substantial frame, made up with a thick comforter and two layers of pillows. A curtain draped along the window, as if it weren't boarded up on the outside. Chase and Keegan lived in an actual home.

Ember passed by the bed. In the furthest corner from the

entrance, a smaller door opened away from her. The closet was deeper than her old room, though not as wide. A string dangled from the ceiling and she pulled it so the naked bulb illuminated the space. Her few belongings had been brought in, folded, and placed on the line of floating shelves.

She stared at it all for a moment. Wondered what it cost. Reminded herself this was Keegan's punishment more than her gain. Temporary.

Ember grabbed a hanger for her coat, set her shoes on the floor, and turned around to study the bed.

It was enormous. She could share it with her mom with room to spare.

Her throat aching, Ember walked to the edge of the wooden frame. Her fingers knotted in the soft comforter, and she pulled. A pillow came along with the cloth. She dragged both into the small closet, and dropped them on the floor.

The door closed behind her. She rearranged her new bed to fill the space wall to wall. Good enough for now. It was better than she'd ever had.

She turned out the light. As she tugged on the down comforter and her head sunk into a ridiculously fluffy pillow, she thought how she'd rather be a little more cold than warm, and how she wished she could hear the murmurs of her mother's barely contained nightmares through her door.

3

NICU

A powerful force thrust against the door of the suite. Nicu hurriedly pulled on his sweater. Tied under the fall of his hair at the nape of his neck, the metal edges of the Trimark medallion caught against the knitted fabric, freezing Nicu's movements.

The folded butterfly pressed into his fingertips as he gently disengaged the angled wing with the curved pentagram at its side. The decorative chains tickled his skin when freed, sending a shiver of foreboding over his shoulders.

He didn't have time to study his response before more heavy knocking echoed through the rooms of the apartment he shared with Branna and Edan. Branna was out on guard duty for the Trimarked Child, and was avoiding him. Though Nicu hadn't seen Edan for five weeks, he doubted the Fae had found his way back into Trifecta, and certainly wouldn't be knocking.

As he left his bedchamber to enter the main sitting area, his features softened, relaxing into non-expression. He rounded the lavishly carved furniture piled with overstuffed cushions and oversized pillows, passing under an elaborate ceiling carving that depicted the celestial sky all the realms shared.

His attention focused on his appearance, ensuring his smoothed braids would keep his secret.

When he opened the thick wooden portal, Wist strode in. Long, white locks fell in juxtaposition against dark cheeks and trailed along the woven pattern of his wrap. An elder of the Fae Council, Wist sometimes took a deeper interest in Nicu. Never comfortable moments; lately their conversations put Nicu on edge, threatening the careful balance Nicu had built between his duty to the Fae and his High Magic Promise to the Trimarked Child.

Wist never hid his displeasure with Nicu's dual loyalties. The Elder had been furious when, at nine years old, Nicu offered Ember a promise. In exchange for keeping away from the humans, he kept her safe. Wist's recent requests of Nicu held the essence of assessments designed to see how far Nicu would go to maintain his balance, and what it meant if he had to choose.

Nicu did not revel in the tests. He refused to fail. Being forsworn to either force in his life was not an option. He had no reason to doubt his conviction. He was more than capable.

"Elder Neyu has told me you brought him concerns," Wist spoke first. The way he curled his lip over the last word held the hint of a sneer that never truly settled into the line of his lips.

"Yes. The humans have changed their behavior," Nicu acknowledged, echoing Wist's own words spoken five weeks ago when the Chaos Star had risen. The Elder noticed, his attention sharpening to the conversation without. The shift suggested he sifted through many thoughts, one of them likely the true reason for this unprecedented visit to a Terraborn Fae's apartment during the pre-dawn hours of the day.

"Is there any sign they are breaking free of the enchantment?" Wist asked, referring to the Fae spell that dampened the humans' instinctive fear of all things magic.

"No."

"Then why the warning?" Wist's question was smooth, though the meaning, sharp.

"Enough of the human children have been banished, or have run away, to the underground Halfer community to truly draw attention to their shrinking population," Nicu explained, his voice flat, his eyes steady on the Elder. "Now they are wondering where these children go. Their curiosity may lead to exploration. As Neyu has added scouts to watch the border, they should know the humans might alter their behavior if they decide to go looking."

"How soon until they send out their search parties?"

"The whispers are new," Nicu acknowledged. "The timeline is uncertain."

Wist's eyes narrowed.

"And how have you come by this information with your new responsibilities?"

"Part of my duty takes me along the town. I have over-heard conversations."

Nicu wondered for a moment if this was the purpose behind Wist's visit. It was likely the Elder had come to ensure Nicu fulfilled his punishment. Not that his new task had been phrased as such.

Nicu had displeased the Fae five weeks ago. When a rogue Wizard cut into Trifecta, the breach in the barrier had caused a direct physical pain along Nicu's spine. In order to stop the pain, he had sealed the cut. The Fae had wished to study the tear, to use it if possible. They had not approved of him putting his own well being ahead of the many.

So they had stripped him of his main duty to guard the Trimarked Child and put Branna in his place. As he was closely connected, they declared, he would be the best to patrol the barrier, to check its status every day and look for evidence of another breach. Throughout each day, he crossed the Pine River, slipped between the trees, scaled the side of the mountain, and climbed the sharp rises along three quarters of Trifecta's boundary. Witch lands were off limits, and that Nicu hadn't been ordered to request access simply solidified the truth of this new task. He was being punished.

Wist studied Nicu's answer. Seemingly satisfied with Nicu's stoic features, he gave a sharp nod. Instead of leaving, though, the Elder moved deeper into the common area. He stopped at the center of the sitting area and pulled an uncomfortably familiar wooden box from his wrap, placing it on the low coffee table.

Nicu let his amber eyes glide over it and back up to the Elder, giving no indication of his accelerated heartbeat.

That box had once held what Nicu now hid, what he had stolen from the labyrinth of treasure-filled tunnels buried deep beneath the Fae compound. The weight of the medallion pressed heavily into his neck.

The folded butterfly wings were latched together now. The metal had been connected to Ember's Binding Ink, a necessary release valve to enable the creation of such a strong spell. To open them would be to release that binding, and Nicu had almost done just that five weeks ago when faced with true danger for the Trimarked Child.

It was Branna who stopped him. Not in words, but in reaction. The Fae had mated the necromancer to Nicu, connected them in order to control the Chaos that surrounded their beings. They had not been told the magic had been tied to Ember's binding as well.

Though Nicu had not used the medallion, he had also not returned it. His reason for collecting it had not changed. The Fae demanded his loyalty. Ember held the power of his Fae given promise. In order to balance both objectives, he needed options.

Nicu counted each breath as he stared into the Elder's dark eyes. He monitored each muscle to remain in posture, to ensure his shoulders didn't tense, or his fingers curl. Silence among Fae held within it a battle of control over truth, and strength of will over secrets.

In the end, it was the Elder who spoke. Wist's words were not a concession, but a change of tactics.

"On a tour of the labyrinth, we discovered this discarded on the floor. The thief did not attempt to hide his crime."

The Elder's clipped remarks betrayed irritation beneath the calm of his low tone. Their contest moved into the conversation, but the rules had not changed. Truth must be chosen carefully. Secrets held deep. Attention honed for every tick that might give the Elder away, just as Wist watched for Nicu's tells.

Nicu needed an obvious question so as not to appear complicit. One the Elder would fail to answer in full. Wist's need to hide his own mysteries worked in Nicu's favor.

"Were the contents dangerous?"

"That would depend on the person who held it."

Nicu allowed his attention to fall onto the box. He'd left obvious evidence, if not a distinct connection to himself. He thought back to that moment weeks ago, knowing he might need leverage in his battle to protect the Trimarked girl and contain her power. Had he been so desperate he ignored the consequences?

"Reckless," Nicu spoke, and the self judgement settled into his soul.

"Indeed," Wist agreed, his nod curt even as he studied Nicu's response. "If the wrong hands happen upon the contents of the box, it would affect Branna in an irreparable manner."

It took every fragment of Nicu's control to hold his body without reaction.

Wist knew the Trimark medallion was connected to Branna.

He was not willing to share with Nicu what the missing relic was.

"I was not informed there was an artifact linked to her power."

"It is not knowledge we prefer to share," Wist granted, voice softened as if he provided a deep confidence out of charity. "If that trinket is activated, it will lead to her downfall. She would turn into a true abomination, no longer of the Fae."

Nicu ignored the Elder's bait. The few heated exchanges he'd shared with Branna convinced Nicu there were no long-term ill effects. Wist could not have noted changes, either, or Branna would not be free to leave Center, much less remain assigned as Ember's guard.

"It needs to be returned." The slight vibration in Wist's voice wasn't what gave the Elder away. It was his word choice.

The treasure needed to be returned. Not found.

Wist knew Nicu took the medallion.

He could not prove it.

Nicu nodded in acknowledgement of the Elder's statement, not in agreement. He allowed silence to fill the room, providing little for Wist to interpret.

Wist drew his posture long. He folded his hands before him in a move reminiscent of the one Nicu had observed five weeks ago in the empty council chamber. There, Wist spoke cryptically about Nicu's choices regarding the Trimarked Child and protecting the Fae from her chaos.

No order had been given, but the conversation had raised echoes of the High Magic that bound his promise. Could the Elder have felt it? Wist wasn't tied to the promise, so Nicu didn't believe so, though the Elder knew enough about High Magic to guess.

"Let us hope the one who took it rediscovers his duty," Wist said. "There is a line here that no Fae should cross."

"I know the importance of duty, Elder." He spoke with a deeper timber, a reminder of the efforts Nicu had employed to solidify his loyalty to the Fae.

"I hope that is true. The thief is mistaken, Terraborn, if he thinks he is above the Elders' judgement. There is not a single Fae with so much import or power that we cannot achieve our goals without them."

Wist snatched the empty box and marched from the room. He controlled the door all the way until it closed with the softest sound.

Nicu filled each corner of his lungs. He counted each beat of his heart until the number was acceptably low. Then he followed Wist out, ready to start another patrol to check on the barrier's status.

4

TRISTAN

Tristan pinched the starfall iron blade between his forefinger and thumb, tracing the shallow channel indented on either side. He'd collected it weeks ago when that idiot Brandt had tried to kill Ember, but dropped the weapon instead. Using speed and a hidden path, Tristan had snatched it off the ground with no one the wiser.

Suffice it to say, the plan with Brandt had failed. Attempting to reach the Trimarked Child these last few weeks proved impossible, as she was always under Fae guard. All he'd gotten for his efforts was colder as the weeks shifted toward winter. His trench coat was enough to keep the chill away for now. If he remained inside this infernal bubble for much longer, he might have to consider something heavier.

The cave he stood in maintained a steady underground temperature, at least. The odd formation was an enlarged bulb at the tip of a long, straight tunnel that had more marks of magic than nature.

A month ago, the saturated power had repelled all life. That was no longer so. His cheek twitched his lips into a smile and he took in the signs. Hair thin growth had broken through the previously barren cave, giving the walls a fuzzy appearance.

They were fast growing babies, too. In the few minutes Tristan had studied them, they'd added centimeters to their invasion. Thicker roots appeared to be breaking through, as well, the rock puckered and ready to crumble against their persistence.

Planted in a dead clearing above where no magic lived, the tiny forerunners were drawn to the thick power in this cave. They drank in the combined powers of the three realms that collected here, an anomaly only found within the Veil bubble.

This special tree was only one part of his plan. Unfortunately, in all his preparation, he had not anticipated a peaceful Trifecta. In fact, he'd made no progress over the last five weeks other than reconnaissance. It turned out the person he needed most for support, his daughter, was far more protected than expected. Little Ember had Fae guardians, Witch check-ins, and even a mixed-blood army whose leader cared enough to hide her.

Not ideal when he'd hoped for race wars to take advantage of.

The Fae, in a move against their nature, facilitated peace. Granted, it was via their magic rather than negotiations, though there were those too. Nineteen years ago, before he'd escaped, there had been talks about drawing up the Laws of Convergence. The Witches pushed hard, but the humans had been skeptical. Then, as it happened, the Fae stepped in.

Leave it to the pixies to manipulate in the wrong way once they broke out their magic wands.

About time he used his, then.

Tristan balanced the knife as he pulled a silk square from his trench coat. He reached to pinch a few fluffy roots from the ceiling, and with gentle motions, wrapped the pieces before returning the packet to his pocket. He would need these for the return trip.

The hilt gripped in his left hand, he squared his shoulders and faced the back of the cave. The curved point of the blade punctured the giving flesh of his right thumb.

Blood swelled into the grooves on the blade. The surrounding power increased in volume, the pressure a physical force against his bones, hungry for the rich energy he offered.

"Take me home."

He struck the spelled knife through solid stone, ripped through thick earth and thin Veil. Light poured into the cave beyond the fissure, but not from magic.

Tristan's moonstone cufflink came to life with the barest thought. He stepped forward and left the dark cavern of Trifecta for a bright, moonlit spring night in his home realm, Heldu.

Twenty years.

Tristan's footsteps faltered. Sweet perfumes shocked his lungs. A full, purple tinged moon glow prickled his skin. His fingers trembled as he lifted his hat from his head and turned his face toward the indigo velvet sky.

If he'd known back then, he would have taken more time to do this, to soak in the beauty and rhythm of his realm.

Or not. If he'd known he'd be forced from his home, he would have fought harder against the Fade, worked longer. Started sooner, so that the last day would have never occurred. He closed his eyes, rebuilt the memory, and relived the day that drove him onto his current path.

}I{

"It's coming!"

Tristan curled his lip. Of course it was coming. They could all feel the magical field roll over and around them, a blanket snapped into the air to dislodge the crumbs caught in its fibers.

Unfortunately, his people were the crumbs.

"Where is High Priest Mindas?" Tristan clenched his teeth and ground his feet as another wave passed through him, distorted his vision as if he were passing through the Veil.

"I'll get him!" a page shouted after the fluctuation. He ran through the open double doors of the Public Hall's library. Tristan's table was situated at the fore of the room, perpendicular to the floor-to-ceiling stacks that tapered out of sight. The ancient archives where Mindas would be found were across the lobby, where they could better maintain the climate for older manuscripts. The runner wouldn't be long. Tristan feared they were already too late.

For three onerous years, Galitti had endured these waves of power. In the last few months, the Fade had come more often. Greater numbers of Witches and Wizards were forced through the Veil, stuck in Terra sometimes for days. So far, they'd returned, but each Fading had been stronger, the Veil stiffer, the passing harder.

"Tristan," the High Priest greeted. The fire red of his hair had grown untended, brown roots echoing the shadows under his eyes. "Do you have news of how to stop the Undoing?"

"I hoped for some from you," he bit out.

With Tristan at the lead, his Coven had refocused all resources to solve the mystery of the Fade. They scoured the tomes and ancient texts for prophecy or aid. He'd assigned Mindas the pages illustrating when the realms had split thousands of years ago.

Humans, Fae, and Witches had all lived together, but distrust between the races became deadly. The Fae had undertaken a great Work and created the Exodus, splitting one realm into three. To Witches escaping human persecution and Fae politics, Heldu had proven more than a haven. The realm was flush with magic. Their people had increased their power and their knowledge in the generations since, much of it kept here at his library in Galitti.

Now the Fade worked to force them back, but only their small portion of the realm. No other Covens had accepted their request for aid. Galitti was on its own.

"Nothing." Mindas gripped his bracelets and twisted them

with rough strength. "The Founders either were not aware the Veil could break, or the Exodus does not hold the answer."

"Leona's scrying—"

"Has produced naught. Which leaves your studies."

"Norri's study of Natural occur-"

"No."

Tristan's lips thinned. He pressed his palms against the pages of notes spread across the table.

"There is nothing," he spoke past the restriction in his throat. "Creating paths is a focused exercise in navigation and discovering the ways to ease through. This is a brute force effort, like someone is using a battering ram against the Veil."

"So it could be caused from outside Heldu." Mindas paled and looked to the ceiling, as if to see the source from beyond.

Tristan drew his fingers in, pages bending and crumpling into his palms. Useless.

Despite their power, their knowledge, they'd only found disappointment.

Tristan's stomach dropped, and he gasped with the force of it. Another wave was coming.

They were out of time.

"Brace yourself!" he shouted.

"So soon?" Mindas spun in a panic and lost his footing with the foreshock of the Fade.

This would be the last one.

"Grab what you can!" he ordered.

All around the extensive library, Witches and Wizards drew as many books as they could hold. Glass cases broke and artifacts were snatched from their displays. Arms and pockets full, some braced themselves against the stacks, others curled onto the floor to protect their precious cargo.

This time, they would not be coming back.

The air pulsed around them. The earth rolled beneath their feet without moving. Tristan closed his eyes, heart snapping as the Fade ripped him from his beloved home. He swore within the pain that he would find a way to re-open the Veil, to return his people to their power-rich world, to escape the muted Terra as soon as he knew how...

}|{

Blood dripped onto the blades of thick, teal grass. The tiny drops were enough to feed earth hungry for it. The plants sprouted and split, rushed forward with a delicate unfurling of seedlings. Tristan curled the fingers of his wounded hand so they brushed the pale amethyst cufflink, bringing healing energy to punctured skin.

There was no sign of the ornate buildings he'd left behind. The domed Public Halls, the curved rooflines of the village homes. The Circle Courtyard that once hosted fairs and celebrations, all dissolved back into the power that created them. Books and tea sets had unraveled, no one there to tend to their creation.

The memory of magic kept it safe. Galitti could be returned to glory soon enough.

He could do it now, even. Or he could stand here forever and soak in the pleasures of Heldu-scented air, wait in this spot for day to rise, and absorb the powerful heat of the sun once it breached the land.

Yet, no wrongs would be righted. No more of his estranged people would find themselves returned home.

There, on the horizon, the Ternate shimmered and reminded him it was time. Five weeks ago, the same group of three stars rose in Terra. Though the realms shared the same planetary space, separated by the magic of the Veil, many differences defined their unique worlds. He stood on a plain, where Trifecta perched on a mountain. Heldu's sky was purple, and starlight filtered through the Universe more slowly, in turn delaying celestial movement.

Five weeks ago, he'd been able to use the power of the

Chaos Star to find a way through the hardened Veil around Trifecta. Tonight, it helped him with a different task.

Tristan marked the beginning of his path. He would need to return exactly here to re-enter the Terran cave. The roots in his pocket would guide the knife. As it was losing its magical coating, he had to limit its use to draw out its effectiveness.

He closed his eyes and carefully plotted his course. Not all Helduans had Faded into Terra. Only those in this geographical space. Only his Coven.

Tristan was not ready to face them yet. Perhaps that day would come when he'd returned everyone from Terra.

To Tristan's magical sense, the threads of power flowed like blood in all living things. The magic within the ground flared to life, eager to be in the skilled hands of a Wizard once again. He spoke his spell, told the bits of invisible energy what to change into and become. A path shimmered before him and around him, and miles turned into steps. The once magnificent grounds of Galitti faded into the wild plains that surrounded it. He strode over rolling hills until he came to a dip in the landscape, a hidden grove tucked into an inverted hill deep enough to hide and guard a small tower.

Aged but sturdy, the structure felt locked in time. The roof of the turret rested below the precipice. He watched the single arched window until he was certain there was no movement within the gloom behind it. Feet turned sideways, he altered his path to carry him down the hill while keeping a careful watch on that singular pane of glass.

At the base of the decline, the great door hung crooked from snapped hinges. Thick vines had sprouted to reclaim land from the building. Tristan hooked his fingers around the worn thickness, propelled himself through the threshold. The hard soles of his shoes clicked in irregular rhythm, each step paced by an abundance of caution.

The single story enclosure that created a rectangle entry beneath the tower was crumbling. Large chunks of stone had tumbled from the wall, reminiscent of a long ago tantrum. Polished tiles on the floor were broken, the rich earth beneath the construction open to the elements. Moss and hearty weeds spread from each point of weakness, their meandering roots traveling via microscopic cracks. To the right, a staircase rose with large sections fallen away.

Tristan was careful not to disturb the rubble as he zig zagged his way up the small flight of stairs. Once at the top, he faced the only object within the entire space still in pristine condition. Golden filigree decorated the edges of the oversized double doors. Flower embossed handles curving delicately where they met. The wood shone as if it claimed a fresh coat of oil. Tristan clasped each of the polished grips, filled his lungs, and pulled.

Despite the powerful movement, no sound marked his entry. No burst of wind flowed out as if seeking desperate release.

Tristan's lips angled into a thoughtful frown. Beyond the doors, he followed the line of the curved staircase until the center of the stone-walled tower blocked his view. Everything within remained fresh, as if construction had completed days ago instead of decades. The stark difference of the spaces left him wondering what awaited him behind that single window set just below the roofline.

To the top, then.

He could not use magic to take the climb. Each stride only devoured two steps, his eyes hooded against the tedious movement.

Tristan reached the upper landing where he stood in a semi-circle ante-chamber. Narrow, horizontal slits peppered the tall wood door at the bisecting wall's center. The peep holes set at different levels and thicknesses held no interest to Tristan, as he wasn't here to observe.

He removed the knife from his pocket and studied the starfall iron. Though thin, the spell that allowed him to cut through magic still coated the blade. He weighed the precision of the weapon against more blunt means, ran his finger over the knife's edge, and decided it would be enough.

Crossing his arm over his body, Tristan sliced through the air in front of the door in a slow, drawn out angle. He muttered a spell to encourage the blade to sever the magical wall built to keep someone in.

No one had thought to guard against a rescue attempt. No one would be stupid enough to let out the Queen, a bane and danger to all Witches.

Desperation, however, was stupidity's more dangerous cousin.

Sweat prickled at Tristan's temples. He frowned, but ignored the irritation as he completed the long stroke of knife and magic. The power of the imprisoning wall proved thicker toward the end, resisting the cut.

Tristan called upon the chaotic energy of the Ternate star, still low on the horizon. The energy of chaos provided the added strength he needed, and the blade slid through to completion.

The door drifted inward a few inches, no latch in place to keep it shut. As he caught his breath, Tristan tucked the knife into his breast pocket, moved forward with tender care, and opened the cell with spindly fingers.

Centered in the room in lotus position, palms open, a girl sat with her head bowed. She wore a pale green gown, silken and smooth, contrasted with the rough weave of a hemp belt decorated with small, watery blue beads. A netted quartz pendant, like a tiny crystal ball, rested against her chest. Reflective moonlight hair flowed over her shoulders, long curtains on either side of an expressionless face. She appeared innocent, sixteen years old. She was much, much older.

Her pose of quiet meditation indicated a docile mind. Of all the souls in this one girl's body, Tristan didn't want calm, but one with a bit more sting. Thankfully, he had come prepared.

Usually, Tristan preferred to use only two stones to guide his Work, both set as his cufflinks. Though he found the duo covered much of the specialized casting he favored, they didn't work in every situation. In an effort to keep away from a plethora of bracelets, he'd figured out other ways to carry certain spell enhancers.

Long fingers pulled at the collar of his trench coat and started counting from the first button on the lapel. One, obsidian. Two, black tourmaline. Three, black onyx. His touch paused there, used the contact to funnel his magic through its crystalline structure to help form and enhance his Work. The trail of power drifted until it settled against the woman on the floor.

Her nose wrinkled. Her ears twitched. Her skin became flushed with a surge of blood. The beads on her waist blurred with color, then brightened and darkened into an angled stripe pattern of brilliant yellow and pitch black.

Her voice hummed in a low, metallic buzz. Lashes raised to reveal the star speckled universe where her eyes should be.

Tristan's body tensed. He greeted the awareness in her gaze.

"Good morning, big sister."

5

NICU

A road fell down the mountain slope and wound into the valley, yet it was a dead end for the residents of Trifecta. It descended to a world below that had forgotten this town existed. Sentinel redwood pines lined each side on raised beds. The faraway city lights blinked across the distance from the valley as the sun rose at Nicu's back.

Dawn at the End of the World.

The place he'd pulled the hybrid girl from the webbing of the barrier. Desperate to free Ember, his tattoos had torn from his skin, a legendary feat only one other Fae proved capable of.

Here, he almost saw his peace end.

He'd almost helped it.

This very place along the border was also where someone had carved their way in through the impenetrable shield, and manipulated a human into attacking the Trimarked Child.

Almost halfway along the arc he checked daily, it had been the catalyst of change. So it became where he started his inspection. After the first few days, he should have changed tactics. It would have been efficient to begin at the Fae-Witch border and travel through the human lands until he reached Witch border again, leaving out the piece of Trifecta pie that was the Circle.

Yet, the End of the World called to him, insisted on imprinting the memory of that night five weeks ago, warning him that though their tale had a beginning, they were far from its end.

He couldn't reverse the healing of the barrier as the Fae requested. If the breach still existed, he could have manipulated his stitching to reveal the cut. Yet, all trace of the point of entry and his long-distance repair was gone.

The edges might have been smoothed when Ember's entire being had become part of the barrier. Likely, the laceration healed on its own. Ember had been forming openings within the wall for her work with the Halfers. Holes did not spatter across the edge, as he confirmed with his daily checks. Either she had closed them, or the Veil magic returned to its stasis form on its own.

It might be either, of course. Nicu would need to question the Trimarked Child to be sure, a strategy shift of enormous proportion. He'd worked for years to understand Ember's skill without knowing what she did. An effort to protect them both as she caused no threat and did no damage. Though he could no longer claim complete ignorance, perceiving too much would prove dangerous, especially now with Wist's suspicions raised. So Nicu delayed the choice.

He was to monitor the barrier. He could resist that order to find her. He was not ready for defiance, or prepared to face her. Not yet.

The power he'd tasted while pulling Ember from the Veil magic had proven feral and violent. Was it her, or was it something else? Was the Binding Ink strong enough to contain it? Or was a massive explosion building in her body?

He didn't know if he could save her.

He didn't know if he should.

The Fae would lock her up, deny her life without attempting to answer either of those questions. Or worse.

The warmed metal of the Trimarked medallion sent a cold

chill down Nicu's spine from where it rested at his nape. Five weeks ago, Wist had suggested Nicu let the dangers surrounding the Trimarked Child move in, to allow fate to decide instead of working to protect her. Nicu had grabbed the talisman in response, had left evidence of it being taken, holding his secret close.

His eyes drifted closed as the sun warmed his back and realization hit his bones.

Wondering what he should do did not matter.

What mattered was what Nicu *would* do. What actions would he take without hesitation? Even knowing the risk to Branna, what would he do if the hybrid girl found herself in danger again? The metal felt warm against his skin, and premonition twisted Nicu's gut.

"Fancy meeting you here."

Nicu's lids eased open. He breathed around the pit that grew in his stomach with the sound of her voice.

"Devi."

"It's come to my attention that your Ink and Ember's Ink may be entirely unique." She spoke as if they were mid conversation and she had caught him not listening.

Nicu remained silent. The Witch invaded his space with more than her noise. Her cranberry curls captured the morning sunlight, bringing a greater brightness to the otherwise pale world of concrete and evergreen trees.

"It would prove beneficial to obtain a pure sample for comparison."

"You are welcome to make your request to the Elder Council, where you can then describe how you got the samples in your possession." It would also take her away from him, his preferred distance from the Witch.

"And where you explain why you let me keep them," Devi challenged.

Nicu raised a brow. He doubted her abrupt appearance

had anything to do with Ink. He played along for the diversion from his thoughts.

"I do not have access to what you ask. I doubt another Fae might donate."

"Even then, just the basic Ink would be preferable," Devi countered. "To see it in its unaltered form, before the bond with your blood changes it."

"No."

"What about Edan? Not Branna, though studying the necromancer is an exciting thought."

"No."

Not to mention Edan wasn't within Trifecta to ask. Nicu's focus passed the energy of the barrier to the world beyond, wondering what his friend had discovered and how long it would take for him to bring the information home.

"Have you found the knife, at least?" Devi shifted her weight to one hip, arms crossed against the chill. A softening of her tone sharpened his senses.

She wanted him to assume she'd distracted him with Ink first, knowing he wouldn't get her access to more. If she hadn't ambushed him at dawn, he might have been easier to convince. What was she after?

"No," he responded, his goal to move the conversation toward her true intention.

Devi lifted the inside of her wrist as if inspecting the small gems held in the delicate hemp webs of her stacked bracelets.

"What about that tracking spell you managed?" she asked.

Nicu drew air into his lungs, focused on the softer sounds of an oncoming winter. The wind, thinner and colder through the trees. The rustle of leaves and creatures readying their food stores and burrows before snow covered the earth. Each tiny, mindful moment to halt the stiffening of his muscles, a visceral reaction to Devi's deceptive statement.

Nicu did not Work magic. That required an ability to harvest raw magical material that he did not have. His skills lay in manipulating energy gathered by another, stealing it for his own. Even then, his spells only lasted as long as he focused them. Once he released his hold, the magic reverted to its raw form.

Ember was different. What he made with her power retained its design, a truth he kept closest, unsure of what to do with it. When he'd caught her sparking in front of that human boy, Nicu released the energy into Nature without it rebounding. He'd been able to use it to separate them from the Veil.

Devi did not need to know any of this, nor did he wish to explain it, not even to play this guessing game of hers.

"You promised me the knife when it was found," she reminded him.

"I did not agree to find it."

"I offered you information."

"Information already owed and given without full disclosure as agreed."

The corner of her lips ticked up.

"Full disclosure cannot come without more data and you assured me I won't get it."

Devi could have been Fae, as clever as she was with words. Her lack of control would have proven a problem, though. He had allowed her theft of tattoo magic structure with the understanding her studies had something to do with Ember, and that she would offer a full report at the end. Her ability to adjust the agreement was impressive.

"Can you prove to me that comprehending Ink is as important as you claimed weeks ago? Or is this to satisfy your personal curiosity?"

"How am I supposed to know without it all?" Devi returned the conversation to Ink, confirmation that neither Ink nor the knife brought her to his side this morning.

Nicu turned from the barrier to face her head on.

"You will tell me, now."

Devi pulled a curl forward to twine around a finger.

"You have nothing to share?"

Nicu narrowed his amber eyes, watched the gemstone green of hers flash over his features.

"Verge," she swore. "I was hoping you knew."

"What?"

"Where Brandt went."

Nicu's nostrils flared on a sharp inhale. He brought in thin, raw oxygen to chill the instinct to move, to stop himself from taking out his anger against the solid air of the barrier with Devi as a witness to his loss of control.

"You let him get away."

Devi dropped her hands.

"That is a strong, unfounded accusation. In fact, someone helped him escape," she bit out.

"A Wizard," Nicu guessed.

"Yes," she agreed with a tilt of her head. "But not one of mine."

Of course not.

"The intruder." Nicu ground his teeth to keep the snap from his tone.

"He has the knife."

"You appear certain."

"Assumption based on the circumstances," she granted. Nicu nodded in acceptance and agreement. Her logic was sound. "We also assume he has Brandt, which is why we failed to locate him."

Nicu studied the Witch. "How long, Devi?"

She shifted to look outside the barrier, a clear break of eye contact.

"He disappeared before the night finished."

The night. Five weeks ago.

Whispers of the humans becoming restless over their runaways disappearing underground, and a person out there whose sudden appearance could be the match to their fuse.

And Nicu had been staring at a wall.

He'd known. The barrier or the girl. What he'd gotten wrong was, he thought he could satisfy both without consequence.

"I appreciate the revelation."

Nicu walked around Devi and headed toward the tree line.

"That's it?" she called after him. Her words faded behind him. Nothing in them encouraged him to respond.

Branna would tell him if anything happened to the Trimarked girl. As she was reluctant to speak to him, she may not have disclosed all events. It was time to end her disobedience, no matter that she was angry with him for not explaining Edan's whereabouts. The hybrid girl's well-being was more important than his mate's grudge.

6

EMBER

$\mathcal{E}$mber had never used a shower before she'd moved in with the Halfers. When she lived with her mother, all she had was a washcloth and cold water from a chipped porcelain sink. She wasn't sure she liked the splashing over her head, but the way the water grabbed the Witch-made soap and used gravity to rinse her clean was a revelation she would never take for granted, no matter how long Chase let her stay.

Or for as long as the Fae allowed her to stay.

Ember increased the heat of the water to battle the chill in her core. The shadow at the edge of the woods fought for real estate in her thoughts, and she considered the chance it might not have been Fae. Slim, given her history.

It had been five weeks. Certainly she was safe after five weeks.

But where was Nicu?

Stop it.

He wasn't, as she'd told Aaron, her constant babysitter. But Nicu had never gone so long without checking on her. She would recognize the weight of his intensity, sense the air shift with pine and mist when he was near. She'd never understood why, but assumed it must be the echoes of a spell the Fae had cast to enforce Nicu's duty to watch over the Trimarked girl. It had been annoying to her, a fly buzzing in her ear. Now, it proved more of a drug, making her twitchy without her regular dose.

Ember didn't remember being trapped in the barrier. Chase told her as much as he could. Nicu had used his physical and magical strength to rip her from the power that held her, a magic so raw in form Devi had sworn it would destroy anyone who touched it. Anyone else.

That implied connection. That implied there was a resonance between them.

And then he disappeared.

Ember turned off the water. Whether it was today or next week, whether he led the Fae to her or watched from the sidelines, she shouldn't waste her time worrying about it. Swallow the fear, keep up the fight. She knew who she could count on.

Herself.

Ember dressed with quick, rough movements, tying her shoes too tight. She'd learned to be one hundred percent ready before unlocking the bathroom door while living with the Halfers. That way, she could escape with short notice if necessary. This morning, at least, she wouldn't have to dodge them. Only Chase, if he was still around. For him, she'd pretend calm, focus on paying him back as much as possible before the Fae had their Trimarked cage ready.

The voices that greeted her when she opened the bathroom door made her glad she'd prepared for a quick exit. She needed to grab her coat from her borrowed room and slip out before anyone claimed it was a good morning.

"I've fed the rumors that Brandt ran away to the underground, but not everyone is buying it."

Wait. Aaron?

Coat forgotten, Ember stepped softly up the hallway, cautious in case it wasn't him. A month had passed since she'd seen or heard from him, after all.

"Even though his dad beat him?" Chase asked. Ember stopped when she saw the pair at the kitchen peninsula. They faced her direction, but hadn't noticed her. Each had a steaming cup of coffee, the cozy scene unexpected after a first meeting where Chase had threatened Aaron.

Aaron ran a hand through sandy curls, a habit she remembered meant he wasn't happy with something. She scowled. As if one day in his forced company was enough time to understand what playing with his fading hair meant.

"Yeah, well. My dad insists Brandt would have come to him, instead of running away. I tried to point out that his friendship with Kyle, Brandt's dad, might have stopped Brandt from reaching out to us, but Dad is convinced that the underground is the last place Brandt would look for help."

"Never mind all the years your father turned a blind eye to what Brandt's dad did," Chase retorted, ignoring the drop of Aaron's attention to his coffee.

Ember shifted, a bitter taste on her tongue with Chase's defense of Brandt. Of course, not every member of his crew were mixed-race kids. Some were humans who came from households that abused them or treated them like they didn't belong because they didn't fit a particular mold. Those were the people Chase's tone spoke for.

Not for Brandt. Not the guy who had spat on her, kidnapped her, and tried to kill her.

"You're doing fine," Chase said. "Enough that someone knocked on my door."

Aaron stared in blue-eyed surprise.

"What did you tell them?"

"What I always tell them. Unless he's the half-breed son of a mage, he can go find someone of his own race to pick on." Chase's lips sharpened into a smirk. "Or something like that."

"Oh." Aaron's fingers spun his coffee cup in a circle. "So... are we done?"

Ember's heartbeat slowed with Chase's small smile. A

familiar static tickled around her bones when his shoulder leaned toward Aaron.

Their movements spoke of familiarity. As if they hadn't spent five weeks apart, or even a day.

"Why, you want to quit now?"

Chase's tone was light, teasing even.

Ember jerked back, a flash of heated emotion burning between her eyes.

Chase had offered to do her a favor, get in touch with Aaron, as if he hadn't spoken to him. Apparently over coffee.

Aaron hadn't visited her, even after protecting her from Brandt. But he kept in touch with Chase. Over coffee.

Aaron had been working with Chase and she'd been dodging Halfer bullies, and terrified over Fae retribution.

She crossed her arms over the twist in her stomach. Her attention flitted between the two guys, her shoulders tense and her appetite gone.

Aaron blushed and stammered over his next words.

"I... I can't help but feel like I failed him and that this is making it worse."

Bright sparks danced in front of Ember's eyes, her power reactive. The light caught Aaron's attention. He paled when he saw her in the hallway.

"Ember!"

She ignored Aaron's shout as she ran through the great room. The front door stuck. She braced her hand against the jamb to pull it open, then slipped through the narrow gap. Her bruised shoulder hit the frame in her rush. A jolt of pain slammed through her body and blackened her vision.

Never mind. She cupped her hand over the injured heat radiating through the knit of her red sweater. Bruises healed.

Ember rounded the house. All the backyards opened to each other, and shared a singular line of privacy fence that bordered the forest, separating yard weeds from the trees. Chase had shown her how to find the scattered loose planks meant as an emergency exit. She squeezed through the gap into an old greenbelt claimed by young redwoods and birch trees. The scent of pine and mist greeted her as the boards snapped into place.

Nicu and Branna stood among the new, thin growth. Branna's fists clenched at her sides, her lips twisted in a snarl. The female Fae used the distraction of Ember's approach to slip into the shadows of the older forest.

Nicu turned to Ember, his face thinner than she remembered. The strength that once encompassed him was now engraved into his bones.

Was this it?

He'd finally come. Unaccompanied by a Fae army, this honed version of Nicu did not need it.

But Branna left furious, so surely he wasn't here to drag her into Center. The necromancer would want to be involved, wouldn't she?

"Little hybrid." The gravel in Nicu's voice scraped her nerves with his displeasure. As if he deserved to be angry, as if his absence hadn't left her unanchored.

Her fingers curled, catching the sparks that escaped. She pulled on weeks of practice gained with the Halfer's and held on to the power. Nicu hadn't noticed, his focus on the wooden panel of the fence that shifted for Chase, then Aaron.

"Reckless." Nicu's charge was so expected, Ember almost released her tension. But his attention wasn't on her. He had directed the word to Chase.

Why was Chase the reckless one?

"It's damn hard to juggle all these balls." Chase shrugged, his hands tucked into his sleeves and his shoulders up to his ears. His breath fogged the cold air, condensed into slow understanding.

"Balls," Ember repeated. "Like Aaron. And me."

Clearly, Chase was more familiar with Nicu than she'd

expected. Maybe even over coffee. Did Nicu drink coffee? She bet Chase knew.

This time, the emotional punch landed against her temple. Chase had seemed oddly unconcerned about the debt she'd been accumulating. Because he owed Nicu something? Or because he was holding her for when the Fae made up their minds?

"For how long?" Her eyes focused on the Halfer who glanced toward Nicu. Ember growled, stepped between Chase and the Fae. This time, he was the one who owed her. She refused to let the Fae interfere. "I'm asking, not him."

Chase studied her face, his eyes hooded.

"He sent me to you five years ago."

Ember's stomach dropped. The barren space filled with pressure.

There was no denying the timeline.

Ember widened her stance, braced herself as the world around her shifted.

The first time she'd opened the barrier, she'd been twelve. Five years ago.

With the Fae, there was no such thing as coincidence.

Ember faced Nicu, saw the truth in golden eyes that refused to waver.

He'd known she could manipulate the barrier.

He'd played to her fear for five years. Upped his game over the last five weeks.

Ember swallowed a powerful need to vomit, her skin clammy.

Nicu had kept her secret for years.

The Fae were not coming.

A deep breath shuttered in, then stuck in her gut.

The fading pixie abandoned her for five weeks, and left her to anticipate which day might be her last.

Nicu stepped closer to Ember. She recoiled, not interested in his closeness, not understanding why he tried to force it. He gestured for Chase and Aaron to step in and tighten their circle.

Ember's nerves prickled, the four near enough to share body heat. Chase stood closer to Aaron who seemed to be half furnace. Ember leaned back to hide the threatening buzz of barely contained sparks.

"I assume there is nothing to report," Nicu began, as if Ember's world hadn't split at the seams. The pressure of a shout built in her lungs, but it was followed by a pressurized ball of power she did not want to let out. She hugged her chest as if fighting the cold rather than the explosion growing behind her ribs, squashing her reaction in order to protect her outer image of control.

"The humans are getting antsy," Aaron responded. "I've been trying to bury the Brandt story, but too many kids have disappeared too close together. They've been knocking on Susan's door, wondering where Ember is, too."

Ember felt the sparks in her palms, focused to keep them there and only there, hidden inside closed fists.

The only reason the humans would look for her is if they suddenly wanted to use Ember's human side. Add her to their numbers in order to tilt the scales in their favor. If they couldn't find her, they'd gain another reason to investigate the underground of Trifecta. A Trojan horse of compassion meant to unearth secrets they'd forced into existence in the first place.

This news had not surprised Nicu. Meaning it was not the focus of this impromptu meeting.

"I hope you are being more forthcoming than Devi." Nicu's voice held a warning that drew goosebumps to Ember's skin. "The Witch informed me Brandt is unaccounted for, and has been for weeks."

Brandt. Free. Out here.

It was too much.

She broke.

Electricity popped. Ember scrambled out of the huddle,

gripped the length of her hair as energy snapped and danced away from her control. The storm clouds above her darkened in response to the heavy pull of her panic.

Aaron came to her side.

"Em, calm down. It's okay."

Said the boy who felt he'd let Brandt down, then dared use her nickname. Ember twisted away from him and the wind kicked up with a howl. Chase reached out, and she moved her shoulder into his path. The energy within her rippled into a second skin around her body and clothes, blocked his touch.

A warm pocket of air eased into her space along with the scent of pine and mist. She should fear Nicu and his connection to the Fae, should be livid. Instead, she drank in the familiarity of her drug, let it become her anchor, reining her mind back from the kaleidoscope of negative energy. She'd never been so lost, so explosive.

Ember did not want this power biting into her blood, threatening to take down the world. She yearned for the containment Nicu offered amidst the chaos trying to escape her, leaned toward his solid presence.

"Breathe." Nicu's order filled her lungs with air. "Where are you bleeding?"

The question caught Ember off guard, broke through the frantic energy of panic to reach her reason. She hadn't cut herself. Had she?

She lifted her hand to cup her throbbing shoulder.

Nicu's breath cut through the noise of the wind, encouraging Ember's own breathing pattern to lengthen along with his. He reached for her hand, hovered without making contact. Tattoos writhed over his skin, absorbed the sparks that jumped from her core.

His movements were efficient without turning sudden, every motion positioned for her to see. Careful and specific. An attempt to defuse a bomb. And as he displayed his control, hers followed.

"Let's see," he ordered. Ember shifted away from him, chest heaving. Nicu followed.

"Blood intensifies magic. You must care for it. Unless you want the storm."

His words weren't quite a question. They weren't quite an accusation.

Thunder shook the air.

Nicu waited.

This is what he did. Stayed on the side lines. Managed from a distance.

Showed up just in time.

With trembling fingers, Ember pulled the neckline of her sweater taut, then slipped it off her shoulder, wincing when the fibers caught the broken bruise. Her pain coincided with a darkening green sky. An eerie silence contradicted the heavy concentration of power.

"Damn that Sadie."

Nicu's golden eyes flickered toward Chase's curse, noted how the Halfer acknowledged how the damage occurred.

"Breathe, little hybrid," Nicu murmured, stepping in once again. His hands hovered, his tattoos swirled. The clouds twisted around one another. "Breathe, or we will be in danger."

Ember's eyes widened. His words had the opposite effect, cutting off her air entirely. Thunder pulsated their chests, reverberated in the air.

Nicu closed the inches between them. His tattoos blackened his thumb. Ember blinked against the specks of light he pulled from the charged air around them, from the storm itself. His tattoos drank in the energy.

Then he touched her. Her lungs unfurled and her skin stitched together as his thumb gently ran across the wound at her shoulder. The magic lightened the blood darkened skin, eased away the pain.

She needs more control.

Nicu's thoughts. In Ember's head.

You never give me any.

Nicu broke contact. Lines of surprise lengthened his stoic features. He blinked them away, checked on the knotted mass of clouds. His tattoos expanded, the muscles along his body bunched. The wind returned in a powerful gust, then settled in as the clouds gradually, naturally, broke apart.

Nicu's tattoos settled into his pores once again, a false life-lessness that mimicked the Binding Ink on the back of her own neck.

"Take care of any wounds right away." The order ignored their exchange of thoughts.

Ember stepped back, her crossed arms a blockade. She couldn't face Nicu, didn't want to acknowledge what just happened. Yet she couldn't look away, watching him from a cautious angle.

He'd caught her with forbidden magic. Again. Fixed it, again. Only to stumble into a new power.

How many of her secrets would he keep? When would that scale tip too far?

Nicu returned to Chase and Aaron who huddled together against the sudden storm. Though wide-eyed, their lack of questions or greater reaction suggested they were adding this event to their collection of confidences, as well.

Verge. They'd become a fading secret society at this point.

"For now, the greatest threat is the human unrest, and that Brandt could ignite it," Nicu spoke softly.

"What?" Ember's brain ached, the edges of her thoughts darkening, their center blurring in a whirl of confusion. "Non-mages asking questions is more dangerous than what I did?"

"Ember," Aaron hissed through his teeth, shaking his head as if to say she shouldn't be reminding the Fae of her power.

"No," she gasped. "I've spent weeks hiding, freaking out over when the Fae would come." Nicu's amber eyes fixed on her pale face. "I'm not going to do that any more. I'm tired. I'm done. How are they a greater threat than me?"

"You call a storm a threat?" Chase asked, brow raised, underplaying the moment. She ignored him, batted back the irritation tightening her throat. His words didn't matter, anyway. They knew the decision was Nicu's.

"I made you a promise." Even with Aaron and Chase nearby, his voice only reached her ears.

The spinning eased and the darkness brightened. Ember stared, speechless, eyes frozen open, fingers twitching against her ribs beneath crossed arms.

Of course she remembered the promise he'd given her when she'd been seven.

If she followed the rules, he would protect her.

"But I broke the rules," she whispered, thinking of all the times she went out with Chase to help with one of his pranks. Opening the barrier. Of her sparks.

"Intentions and purpose matter. Nothing you have done threatens the Fae."

Nausea froze, breath coiled. She'd grown up with Nicu, and understood nuances. He'd just told her she was in direct competition for his loyalty.

"Keep her close," Nicu ordered Chase, the boy he'd sent five years ago as added protection. "Act as if she does not have a Fae guard. And keep a hold of your fading Halfers."

Chase startled with the force behind Nicu's last words, and nodded in response. Ember stared at his disappearing form, uncertainty shifting her feet.

A storm might not be threatening to the Fae, but if her power kept growing, how much longer until he chose his people over her? He'd protected her so far, bound by the power of his Fae promise, making her wonder if he might choose to protect her over the demands of the Fae, instead, in order to satisfy that bond.

Ember's head split, her brow wrinkled, stomach wringing her apart.

She needed air. Air she didn't have to share with another person.

"You don't have a coat," Chase called as she walked, unseeing, into the trees.

Because, of course, it was his job to 'keep' her.

"I'll come back when I'm cold."

A promise and resignation. Because Nicu's promise to her had strings attached. One tied to each of them.

7

NICU

The energy of change slithered over Nicu. His nerves twitched, trying to escape the feeling he'd rather ignore. He shook off his brief loss of control with Chase. The extra energy in his parting words did not matter in the face of the morning's true challenge.

The reason he'd given Ember to explain why he kept her safe, invoking the promise, had been a deflection.

He'd always been certain if the world broke, it would be because of the Trimarked Child.

His interaction with her and the barrier last month convinced him of her potential strength. Her lack of control supported the world would end by fire.

Yet, he could not deny the growing evidence, could not ignore that each time she flared, he managed her power as any other Fae managed the magic of Nature.

His healing of Ember had not undone itself. His release of the storm sent it drifting away.

Her power. His control.

And they'd somehow shared thoughts.

The nausea that rose within him as he entered Center was unexpected. He swallowed it down, nevertheless. The Fae would be disappointed because they did not understand. Nicu believed in his path and choices. He could still do his duty for the Fae. Keeping these secrets protected them from the chaos of this realm, allowed them to live peacefully, and protected them from taking action based on unfounded fear.

The Fae would not approve, but they did not have to know.

Years of practice letting emotions pass through without a physical reaction allowed Nicu to refocus himself. Deep breathing reset his heart rate. Gentle urging directed his working thoughts to each step his body made. He concentrated on the rising of his thigh, the descent of his foot, the pressure against his heel, the power of his toes.

Self-discipline gave him room to prioritize. His entanglements with Ember would be sorted later. For now, he needed to speak to Branna, to gain her aid in finding the human, Brandt.

Focusing on what he could control gave him greater command of his actions.

Nicu kept to the edges of the courtyard, working to stay out of sight without appearing to sneak. He rarely had reason to be within Center at this time of day. He preferred not to draw attention to the change.

An old shed disguised the entrance to the Fae apartments. The heavily fortified building had been decorated to blend in with the artisan enhancements of the upper village, but otherwise left to appear as a shed.

Inside proved utilitarian at first glance. Rakes, shovels, and other maintenance equipment lined the carved, live-edge shelving along each side. The organized shelves allowed plenty of room to walk toward the back. From there, he passed through a hidden door and descended the elegant, spiral staircase.

In true Gypsum, the Upper Fae would never live below ground. Such accommodations were saved for servants or prisoners. In Terra, however, safety had been at the forefront of the Council's mind. After conferring with the magic of the area, underground proved the most accommodating for housing. The village above was a suitable distraction for potential visitors, though so far there had been none.

The lower halls were not dank or confusing like the treasure tunnels one layer down. In contrast, each wheel-spoke hall was marked with relief carvings of different flowering vines along their lengths. Reverent knives brought the images to life before the carvings had been stained in realistic shades. Artisans had laid the polished pine that lined the squared walls out in a clearing for thirty full moon nights in order for the lumber to soak in the soft glow. The stored light now lit the halls with a gentle presence.

Nicu chose the Path of Daisies until he reached the arched doorway of his suite. The lighter birch doors had not been spelled, though the shift of wood tone created misty looking portals.

Inside, the walls were the same illuminated pine with thick, rich curtains gathered in each corner, waiting to be pulled closed to dim the enchanted wood. Branna spread out on the singular couch. The white upholstery contrasted her woolen sweater and fitted joggers, both black. She stared at the constellations decorating the ceiling, ignoring his presence. Nicu eased his way toward a low chair, stood behind it, his hands pressed into the delicate scrollwork of the backrest.

"Branna."

"Unless you are going to fill me in on Edan's whereabouts, I have nothing to say to you."

Nicu did not allow his fingers to tighten their grip.

"I do not know where he is."

Branna's tattoos settled like boxing tape around her knuckles as she sat up.

"That is very Fae of you, to tell me the truth in such broad terms," she accused. "You sent me away that night for a reason."

"To escort Susan home."

The argument had been repeated many times these last few weeks as nothing changed. Until today. Nicu steeled himself against Branna's heated stare.

"I should have assigned you to the human, seen if your shadow stalking skills extended to the Witch lands."

Branna tilted her head. The smooth top bun she wore kept firmly in place. This was as close as Nicu came to admitting a mistake. She would not give in by asking for further explanation, though. He would have to bridge the gap further.

"As I tried to tell you before the Trimarked Child interrupted, Brandt has disappeared."

"Recently," she assumed.

"That night."

Branna pet the feathery edges of her scythe-curved tattoos as if they had texture different from her skin.

"I have asked the spirits many times for the soul count within Trifecta." Her reluctance to engage with him drew her words long. "All deaths were accompanied with cremations."

So she'd been checking to see if Edan had died. Nicu breathed around the realization. He didn't believe her actions stemmed from a lack of trust in him. Her confession betrayed her depth of feeling for the other Fae.

Nicu and Branna had been mated by the Fae in an attempt to wrestle some control back from the chaos of the Trimarked Child's disastrous entrance into the world. Chaos had as much hand in the Fates as control, however, a truth Nicu faced every day with his duty to the hybrid girl.

Nicu had known for years that Branna's feelings did not support their match, a matter that held no consequence for him besides relief. Her undeclared choice absolved him of a responsibility he did not have the capacity for, yet it set a different expectation of loyalty.

Nicu would find a way to ease Branna's concerns without giving away the full truth, a minor concession to gain her aid.

Branna held no love for the Child Nicu was sworn to. She would need a different motivation.

"Edan is in a place of his own choosing." Nicu's voice drifted only as far as Branna's ears.

"Then I am angry with both of you."

Not the desired response, but one possible to work with.

"There is a gull to be found," he enticed her with the Fae slang for human, a sign this would be a hunt. "Delicacy is not required."

Branna's tattoos shifted again. Though the frequent movement was unusual for the necromancer, Nicu was unwilling to press their fragile truce by noticing.

No matter that Wist's warning oozed like an illness into Nicu's thoughts. Nicu was prioritizing Brandt. Ember would come later. Branna, he would watch, but not as his primary objective.

After a few breaths of silence, Nicu expected Branna to refuse him. He calculated other offers, but then she swung her feet to the floor.

"And I deliver him to Devi."

Negotiation. Good.

Nicu lifted his lips in a smile that held her answer.

Branna flashed her teeth. With a blur of black, she slipped through the door, leaving Nicu to catch up.

8

EMBER

*E*mber was so fading tired.

The sun rose high enough to melt the frosted crystals, the day barely begun. Yet, exhaustion blanketed her whole self.

Life had been easier a month ago. Just her mom and her, struggling but making do. Running with Chase's crew for a bag of food or new clothes. Knowing Nicu or one of his unit lurked in the shadows somewhere.

Relationships were linear. Limited. Understandable.

On her terms.

That had been her truth, until she learned everything had been driven by a Fae's promise.

She tried to clear her mind, emulate the Fae who she resented and needed. As always happened these days when she didn't plan her footsteps, Ember found herself within shouting distance of home.

No. Not home anymore.

Her mom's house.

Ember dragged her feet past the last few trees, careful to stay deep enough she wouldn't be seen. Not that the chance was high. Susan never left. The only window was in the front door. The back wall was solid cinder block construction.

"I've been keeping an eye on the place."

Ember faced the source of the noise as she backed up, fists raised in defense.

Aaron stood a few feet away. An outstretched hand offered her something black and plush. His even breathing suggested it hadn't been difficult for him to catch up, though his loose jogging sweats and tight fleece zip-up were ready for exercise.

"How did you know where I'd be?"

"I followed the trail you left. Chase caught up to give me your coat. He didn't think you'd want to see him right now."

Ember narrowed her eyes toward his last mumbled words, pretty sure she didn't want to see Aaron right now, either. He seemed clueless, and shook the coat to remind her to take it.

"You two are getting along nicely," she challenged.

Aaron's cheeks warmed, and he rose on his toes before dropping to flat feet.

"I owed Chase a favor." Aaron gestured toward his thigh where Brandt had stabbed him. "I guess being healed by a Halfer is expensive."

Which might have satisfied her, except for what Ember overheard in Chase's kitchen. Aaron hadn't seemed eager to leave the partnership then. He wasn't sure enough humans bought his Brandt the runaway story.

So she had people to look out for her, but for what reason? Nicu had a promise to keep. He'd given Chase a job. Chase had given Aaron a job. It was difficult to dredge up gratitude for those motives.

She turned from him toward Susan's house, though she didn't register any of it, caught blind by a fog of anger and anguish.

"She gets the food left for her. Sometimes she cries, most of the time she doesn't." Compassion coated his soft words. "She's started stepping out. I thought she watched the sunset, but she seems to be looking for someone. Something that scares her, I guess, since she jumps at any noise."

Ember wrapped her arms around her waist and dropped her eyes. Was her mom looking for her? Afraid of her?

"More of your orders?" The words bit at her lips. Aaron's flinch showed he felt the sting.

"No. I thought you'd want someone to watch her with everyone else keeping tabs on you." He shrugged. "Do you want me to stop?"

So it wasn't all because of what he owed Chase. She'd forgotten how fading nice Aaron was. His well meant actions sent a soothing wave over her stiff defense.

"No. Just. Don't let her catch you."

The light that brightened his eyes reminded her of a hopeful puppy, his curls bouncing when he lifted his chin with a smile and held out the blob of black fabric.

Ember accepted her coat. As she put it on, she turned away from the stupid normal boy with his expressive features who kept an eye on a complete stranger he must think was crazy. That he'd chosen to proved the breaking point for Ember. How could she stay mad when faced with Aaron's selflessness? He didn't have memories of Susan's good times. He didn't have memories of her as a caring mother. Aaron couldn't understand how Susan broke under the devastation of knowing the world hated her daughter. How the taint of magic, however unintended, was too much for her fragile mind.

Verge, who could?

A breeze flowed past, brought by the wind rather than her temper. Heavy clouds blocked the sun and shadows deepened under the trees. The memory of seeing someone in the forest last night flitted across her mind. After what she'd learned from Nicu, it wouldn't have been the Fae. Her breath expanded her ribcage and a few joints cracked with the release of tension. Could it have been Aaron, another time he'd been close without reaching out?

"When do you come by?" Ember asked.

"Whenever I run in the morning, I loop past here, then go up into the forest. It hides when I meet with Chase. In the afternoon, while dad watches TV after dinner, I sneak over through the woods at the front." His gesture down the hill echoed his words.

Ember frowned. So the shadow hadn't been him. Had she imagined it?

Without anything to anchor her worry, she let the mysterious figure go. Another part of Aaron's explanation rose to the surface. He'd spoken of his rendezvous with Chase without hesitation. When she'd led him underground, he'd been uncomfortable around the unfamiliar Halfers. Now he was so acclimated he was taking meetings with Chase. But she was the one he wasn't comfortable enough with to say hi to. Then why was he here? Why did he watch Susan?

"How." Ember clenched her teeth together, determined not to ask. Aaron shifted toward her, cocked his head and focused those fading curious eyes on her.

"What?" How could he pose such an open question without guile, without deeper meaning?

How was Ember supposed to resist?

"How often have you met with Chase?"

Aaron shrugged as if it were no big deal. "Every couple of days or so."

Ember slowed her breath, refusing to acknowledge the heat in her chest.

She did not want to ask. The words came anyway, compelled to release the pressure, no matter the consequences.

"You didn't come see me."

Ember refused to peer at Aaron, refused to let whatever expression that crossed his emotive face mean anything to her.

"Of course, it was only a day," she rushed. "And it wasn't like we became friends. Close."

"Em."

"No. It's fine. Forget it."

Aaron's arms surrounded Ember's stiff form. His warm breath heated her chilled hair.

"What are you doing?" she whispered, seizing the power of the barrier, not wanting her sparks to nip at him.

"Apologizing."

"Why?"

Aaron huffed in frustration and eased from the attempted hug.

"Because I'm a jerk. I didn't think you wanted to see me. I hoped that if I did this job for Chase - a job I had to fight for, by the way - you might hear about it and come find me."

"I thought this was all because you owed Chase."

"Two birds." Aaron tucked his hands in his pockets and settled into his natural stance, bouncing on his toes. "I also thought it best to choose my own form of payment."

He was getting good at dealing with the magic world. Ember's eyes narrowed, not finished with him.

"And are the lies you spread why you feel like you failed Brandt? Because now you're helping keep what he did a secret?"

Aaron hunched his shoulders, and a crease formed in his brow.

"No. I should have helped him sooner, stopped all of this. But I'm helping because it's the right thing to do. You and I have had someone who should have protected us, stab us instead. In your case it's figurative, but you get what I mean."

For a moment, Ember did not understand his conclusion. When she glanced at the solid grey of her old home, the pieces fell together.

Brandt had stabbed Aaron in the leg. Ember's mom had wounded her heart.

"You have no idea what you're talking about." She choked on the words, her volume drained along with her desire to fight.

"All I wanted to do is help." Aaron reached out as if to grab Ember's hand. She flinched, but he never made contact. She released her hold on the power enough for a flicker of blue to flare between their skin, keeping them millimeters apart.

"A literal defensive wall," he muttered with a frown. "What did Devi do to get through it?"

"Devi?" Ember jerked. What did the Witch have to do with anything?

"I don't know why you went to her last month, but I know it was for some kind of help."

"And that gave you the idea that we're what? Friends?"

Aaron's brows drew together. "Yes?"

Ember's bark of dry laughter startled a squirrel into chattering back.

"Not even close. You see, Nicu follows me around, making sure I don't break the rules. The Coven lets me have a little more freedom as long as I check in with Devi once a week. And yeah, this time I had a problem, but usually I'm just her research project. She casts a quick spell, takes notes, and releases me back into the wild."

An emotional wave rolled over Aaron's features. Eyes wide, lips parted. Lashes narrowed, lips thinned. Then a twinkle in his eye and a smile.

"So I'm your first friend."

Ember coughed through her surprise.

"We knew each other for a day," she challenged.

"An eye opening day."

Right.

Ember stared at Aaron until he rocked between his toes and heels. He glanced over his shoulder, then sighed.

"Okay. Well, now that we're talking to each other, let's meet later? I have to get my run in before I head home."

Was he making plans with her? There was no response.

"Please?" He all but fluttered his eyelashes.

She might have almost smiled in reply.

"We'll see."

Aaron puffed a cloud of warm breath into the chill day. "Okay, fair enough. I'm still going to try, though."

Ember rolled her eyes with a dramatic lift of her chin. Aaron laughed and broke into a backward jog. With a wave, he turned up the hill and headed deeper into the woods, parallel to the line of houses and back toward the Halfer zone.

He took his ease with him, leaving Ember with her heavy heart and weighted thoughts. This day sucked, and the morning was only halfway through. Everything was so out of control.

Fades, was she channeling Nicu, now?

That didn't make it untrue.

Not that there was much she could do about it. She couldn't break Nicu's need to control. She couldn't change Chase's obligations. She surely had no impact on Aaron's... whatever it was.

At least she was away from the Halfer crowd. That was one complication gone.

There was something she could control.

Herself.

More specifically, her power over the barrier.

She'd managed the shield around her skin with Aaron on purpose. Maybe there was more control than chance with the way the Veil magic closed.

Her fingers shook, her head began to pound. She shut it all down.

She could do this. She could at least get time in, repetition to help ease the anxiety.

Five years ago, she'd taught herself how to manipulate the barrier through trial and error and secret practice. She hadn't let fear stop her, then. Could she do that again?

Nicu had said to act as if she didn't have a Fae guard.

Chase wouldn't be coming after her, not for a while.

But.

Brandt was out there. There was one more player, too. The Wizard who helped him was also in Trifecta. If Brandt had been missing for five weeks, they might be together, hiding. Waiting.

More things she couldn't control.

Likely, if Fae and Witches hadn't found them, she wouldn't stumble on them by accident. Besides, she wasn't helpless. She'd trained more with Keegan these past weeks. She'd eaten better, gained strength. The stranger was more interested in talking to her than hurting her. She won her first fight with Brandt.

Verge, she'd been on her own for seventeen years. How did a month of being pampered by Chase lead to this debate?

Enough. Ember made her way down the hill, her destination the vacant stretch of land north of Town, east of Center. The thick forests were almost always empty, a safe haven for a girl who had nowhere else to go. Her original practice ground, and the place where she'd discovered her secret all those years ago.

9

AARON

*A*aron jogged through the forest, cut the edge of Witch lands and then back to the manicured roads of the human neighborhood. Crossing the Witch boundary put a reckless smile on his face. Even though the bubble held firm, the fact that he felt safe enough to run on Witch land had made his little space in this world one hundred percent bigger. Imagine if he figured out Fae land.

Aaron remembered Nicu's forceful grip on his neck. Twice. Never mind. He'd stick to Witch lands. One hundred percent bigger was plenty.

A month ago, he hadn't even known the exact location of the boundaries. Chase taught him how to find the vines that wrapped through the trees as the mages' equivalent of a high security fence. The triangular leaves lining the Witch border were curled and brown now, making their discovery difficult, but not impossible.

A bigger world, thanks to Ember.

Aaron wasn't sure what it was about this morning's conversation with Ember that put a smile on his face. She'd melted a bit. The hint that she'd missed him was incredible. During his attempted hug, her magic shield hadn't popped up, though it had later when he'd reached for her hand.

Now that he and Ember were talking, Chase couldn't stop him from visiting, no matter when Operation Lie About Brandt finished. Aaron looked forward to their morning coffee, to Chase's quiet, forceful energy. Chase had even confided in him a few times, let slip who his mom was, then sworn Aaron to secrecy.

Aaron had agreed without hesitation. Now that he recognized mages were just other people - weird people, granted - more of his world opened up beyond possible running trails. He didn't want to risk losing it over a spilled secret, or because of a mission ending.

Aaron wove his way up the rectangular grid of the human neighborhood and headed toward the Saturday market along the lower streets as part of that assignment. Trifectans used an old single story strip mall as a gathering point for trade. Booths of different sizes were set up in grids inside large rooms that had once been a grocery store, a few restaurants, and a hardware supply shop. The races were intermixed in accordance to the Laws of Convergence so none of the races were singled out or ignored. Each group had two booths next to each other for comfort, the booths on either side being of a different race to ensure inclusion.

Witch booths were the most popular. Hand-sized bars were stacked and labeled as soap, conditioner, or lotion. Glittering glass bottles were filled with toiletries, cleaners, or wine. Fragrant honeycombs were sectioned and wrapped in wax. Rainbow mounds of produce filled baskets and crates. They also brought salvage from their renovation projects.

The Fae booths were busy, but no one lined up. Buyers did not browse, but quickly selected their items, then left. They offered wild game on ice, cut and wrapped in beeswax cloth. Wood creations drew the eye and sparked imagination, whether from trinkets or heavy furniture. Sometimes a brave human bartered for personalized hand carving services on items they already owned.

Human-run booths were littered with clothing for trade, mostly smaller childrens' items. Mending or alterations could be left for later pickup, though a button could be replaced while the customer waited. Other sellers offered small item repairs, and appointments were made for in-home needs. Smaller boxes of produce and eggs were available from back-yard gardens. Knitted clothing and other handmade items were artfully displayed, pieces competing with Witch items for the discerning human buyer.

Gus preferred to steer clear of multi-race meeting points, so he and Aaron rarely visited the market. As a teacher and coach, Gus' pay comprised all living resources, and he arranged to have them delivered to the house. The last few weeks, however, Aaron ran through each Saturday to listen to the gossip of the adults after working his human-style magic around the Brandt story at school.

As he jogged through, people he made eye contact with gave him a soft wave hello, but didn't gesture him over. No one called his name, offered him a free sample while they not-so-subtly asked about his friend.

Instead, they watched him with side glances, turned conversations so at least one person had a view of him as he passed.

A heavy knot tightened in Aaron's stomach.

Something had happened.

For the last month, they'd practically begged him for some insider knowledge he was supposed to have because he'd been Brandt's best friend.

Now they looked uncertain of him.

"Aaron." Aaron jerked from his thoughts and found Paul catching up to jog along, not bothering to ask him to stop.

Having been the soccer captain before he graduated last year, Paul knew Aaron's dad, a.k.a. Coach Gus, wouldn't hesitate to reprimand him for interfering with his new captain's training schedule.

"What's up with everyone today?" Aaron asked.

"No one told you?" Paul gaped. "Nancy Powell disappeared."

"The junior?" Aaron asked with a frown, recalling the name from school.

"Yeah. That makes three who fell off this month alone. Everyone is tightening restrictions. No car rentals for the teens right now. No End of the World party tonight." Paul looked behind him to check their distance from the market, as if the entire town wasn't already talking about this and he wanted to keep it quiet. "They think she went underground."

"Why?"

Paul shrugged. "There's no other option. The pixies and gnomes wouldn't take her." Aaron ran a hand over his face to hide his flinch at the slang for Fae and Witches, a reaction he wouldn't have had a month ago.

"No, I mean, why did she go?"

"My girlfriend says there is a rumor going around school saying she's pregnant."

"Her parents kicked her out?"

"Verge if I know," Paul muttered. "They claim they're as shocked as everyone else."

Aaron slowed to a walk and Paul followed.

"Sorry, I didn't even ask what you wanted to talk about," Aaron said.

Paul cleared his throat and licked his lips, his eyes trailing back toward the market.

"The thing is... Brandt—"

Aaron picked up his jog again, moving away from Paul, who cursed under his breath and caught up in a few strides.

"Look, this has got to be hard on you, everyone bugging you for information. But this girl is pregnant. It's different."

That went from rumor to fact real quick.

"How long has she been gone?"

"A few days. I'm honestly surprised you hadn't heard."

Aaron's lips thinned. He'd been too busy fueling rumors of his own to pay attention to others.

"Anyone saying who the father is?" Aaron asked, a theory forming. She was young, but babies were few and far between these days in Trifecta. If her parents hadn't kicked her out on a moral basis, why would a girl leave home just for being pregnant?

"No one's come forward, and Nancy isn't here to say. Why is that important?"

Chase had very specific reasons he'd accept someone into his Halfer family. One exception, someone carrying a Halfer baby.

Fades.

"I don't know where she is," Aaron answered truthfully. Chase didn't keep him updated on Halfer members. With these questions, the caution was justified. "The dad might, though."

"And there's no way to find Brandt, even to say if they're in the same place." It wasn't a question, it was resignation. Paul, at least, believed Aaron on that point. "Thanks, man. Tell Coach I say hi."

"Yeah. Thanks. And sorry."

"Nothing to apologize for. It's not you hiding these kids."

Paul's swift departure meant he missed the blood drain from Aaron's cheeks. He took in a deep breath, blurred vision not great while jogging.

He wished this had happened before his morning meeting. At least he had plans with Ember, kind of, and that might offer him a chance to update Chase.

Aaron picked up the pace and headed uphill toward home.

He slowed to a walk when he reached his street, then moved through a few stretches on his porch before heading inside.

Gus wasn't in the basement gym as expected. Aaron heard his voice in the kitchen and rounded the central staircase to check out their visitor.

Aaron's step hesitated as he crossed into the kitchen, taking in the two men already there. His dad glanced at him but didn't otherwise acknowledge his presence to introduce him to the stranger sitting on a low-backed stool. Gus leaned against the island, dressed in loose shorts and a long-sleeved t-shirt.

Across from Aaron's dad, the stranger sat upright as if his vertebrae were fused into a straight line. A trench coat open to a three piece suit, an odd choice of clothing given there were no formal events planned. A black hat with a small valley through the top rested on the pale granite, his fingers spider-like where they perched on the cool stone countertop.

"Have you talked to Brandt's dad, Kyle?" Gus was asking.

"I tried, but he wasn't very receptive," the stranger tried to soften his words, but irritation sharpened their edges.

"Yeah, that's Kyle," Gus confirmed.

Aaron moved quietly as he grabbed water, an apple, and a hand towel to mop his sweat, careful to give space to the two men. He watched the pair from the corner of his eye.

"It's a shame," the stranger said. "I was hoping since you were friends with someone who had gone underground that it might help me find my sister."

"She's a runaway, too?" Gus asked.

"She's more impulsive in her choices. In fact, she may have returned while I was gone, but it's been a few hours since our fight and she threatened to disappear." The stranger's voice spilled like oil, slippery, cold, and disconcerting.

"I'm sorry. Can you describe her? Aaron here runs the town. He can keep an eye out for her."

Aaron bit into the apple a little too hard, wiped his mouth with the back of his hand to hide his reaction. Was this one of the three Paul told him about, or someone new? He flipped around and leaned against the sink. The stranger's lips angled up in a sharp smile.

"How kind. She's a slight girl, about sixteen, with pale hair. She finds it hard to stay still and fidgets."

"Is she a sophomore?" Aaron asked, struggling to fit the description with the girls at school.

"Oh, she doesn't attend Trifecta High. She becomes disruptive if confined for long. We have been homeschooling her as best we can. We have a house at the bottom edge and she's able to wander the woods, but she usually stays close to home. A creature of habit despite her oddities. That's why I'm worried."

"Well, if she's predictable, why don't you get back in case she shows up? We'll keep an eye out up here for you," Gus promised.

The stranger turned muddy green eyes to Aaron, his head tilted at the top of his long neck.

"Was it your friend who ran away? Can you reach him to discover if my sister is underground?"

A popular question these days. Aaron exaggerated his chewing movement, motioned that he couldn't talk with food in his mouth.

Gus shifted his body. His eyes sharpened with warning as his fingers laced together and his knuckles paled.

Aaron made a show of swallowing.

"I haven't talked to Brandt in five weeks. I have no idea if he's underground or managed to fall off. The jerk hasn't said a word to me."

The magnitude of that statement sank from his lips to his shoulders. Brandt hadn't reached out. Devi admitted the Witches lost him before the night turned to day.

Where the verge was his friend? Ex-friend. What the verge was he doing?

"Oh. I must have misunderstood the talk around town. I thought you were telling your friends at school where he was."

"You heard wrong. Or people are getting mixed up. Brandt got mad, shouted a few things, and disappeared. One of them was a threat to run away."

Gus' eyes widened, and he cleared his throat.

"Anyway." Gus straightened and gestured for the stranger to follow him to the front door. "What's your name again?"

The man answered, but Aaron had trouble hearing through a soft, musical buzzing in his ears. A heavy fatigue drained his ability to focus. The run through town had taken it out of him. Was Gus at the door? Who was the strange guy talking to him from the porch?

"If we see her, we'll send her down the hill."

"I'd be very thankful," the man responded. Gus closed the door. He hadn't even let the guy in or offered him a drink. Must not have been important.

Aaron shook the fuzz from his brain and took another bite of his apple.

A moment later, Gus leaned in the arch, arms crossed.

"What else did he say?"

Aaron's cheeks bulged with food and he winced when the oversized lump scraped his throat.

"Who?" Aaron asked, sifting through the last few minutes. Had they been talking about something before that guy knocked on the door?

"Brandt. What did you leave out of your story?" Gus' lips were soft in their frown, his eyes intent. "You said he yelled a lot of things when he left that night. Did he talk about hurting himself? Then or ever?"

Aaron tried to catch up with his dad, vaguely remembering questions about Brandt. He filled his glass again, hoping the water would cut through his strange, post-workout headache. The conversation wasn't coming back, but Brandt hadn't ever said anything about hurting himself, so why—

Fades. His dad thought Brandt killed himself.

Aaron paled. Could Brandt have killed himself?

Would the Witches have killed him and covered it up? Would they tell Devi if they had?

Or was Brandt's mysterious Wizard helping him?

"Dad." Aaron choked, his eyes wide, shoulders bent. "I mean, no. Not like that. He was angry. He drank. But he never talked about that."

Gus nodded and looked away, then ran a hand through his hair.

"Yeah. Okay. Maybe I need to find this underground. To make sure. If he's there, fine. Curiosity satisfied. He might come back if he knows he can stay here. If he's not, we'll have to search - We'll talk about that later."

Aaron gagged, turned to bend over the sink. Pieces of fruit threatened to erupt from his stomach. He coughed to clear the pressure and finished what was left of his water.

"Hey, son," Gus appeared at his side. "I'm sorry. I'm sure he's fine. I just want to see it for myself."

"Y-yeah, I get it,' Aaron rasped. "And you're right. We should check."

He'd have to warn Chase to take a softer touch with his dad, but they'd work it out. Then Aaron would have to search for Brandt. Again.

"Do you know where to start?" Gus asked. "Is there a secret code passed between the kids?"

"N-no, I don't, but I can try to find out. It might be better if I do it, anyway. The Halfers aren't likely to let an old topsider down." Chase would prefer that, too, being able to control the contact.

"Old?" Gus asked, a brow raised in an attempt to bring humor to the conversation. Aaron forced a smile that moved his cheeks but never reached his eyes.

"Practically a mummy," he agreed. "I'll look this weekend."

"Okay. If you don t find anything, I'll bug the town council.

It might be time to engage these kids, make them talk. At least to tell us who's with them."

Chase would weld shut all the doors first, but it wouldn't help to explain that to his father. Aaron's plan had a better chance. He just had to get to Chase.

Aaron ran upstairs to grab a shower before heading out again, no longer convinced he was glad his world had gotten bigger.

10

EMBER

Sweat misted Ember's skin despite the brisk temperature. She looked around her, certain of her solitude. She'd spent years learning when she was being watched or not. So far, so good. She would keep checking.

This area of the forest, though human territory, was where the Fae did much of their hunting. Officially, anyone could hunt, but the humans left the Fae to the task to allow them to 'earn their place.' Ember believed it was because bows and arrows, the Fae weapons, were easily replaceable. Human bullets and the materials to make them were impossible to get into Trifecta. Why waste finite ammo on food when you can horde it in case of a war?

Not a helpful thought, with what she'd learned this morning about the humans becoming restless. If they decided to search the forest for runaways, at least humans were loud and she'd hear them coming in plenty of time to hide.

It was the Fae that worried her, with their silent movements and ability to blend. Nicu kept her secret. It would be incredibly irresponsible to be caught by a random patrol.

Ember was alone now, though. Being watched settled

heavily in her consciousness, and she felt free of that particular pressure. She was safe from the Fae, at least.

She thought she was safe from the barrier.

She just didn't want to touch it.

Which was ridiculous, because she'd been nervous but fine last night. Granted, Chase had been there along with the pressure to not disappoint, and to pay toward her debt to him.

Now she only had herself, and she froze.

Get control of yourself.

The words might have been Nicu's. The mental voice was hers.

Ember huffed air through pursed lips and squared up to the barrier.

She could do this.

She raised her fingers, held her breath, and tapped.

The barrier rippled and the opening's edges sparkled blue, like the power that came from within her. The rest of the dome remained invisible even to her eyes.

Magic didn't attack, but waited with her. Paused to see what might happen.

Ember's hand trembled, and she reached forward, wondering if this meant she could pass.

But no. Her fingers stopped, not against the pressure of a wall, but with the magnetism of not belonging. Other people and bags of food passed through, but Trifecta held her.

She let out her breath. The gap closed.

That made little sense. The power wouldn't respond to her oxygen use. What else had she done?

Open. Waited. Released expectations.

Oh.

Oh!

A rush of fiery blood erased the autumn chill from her skin. She licked her lips and reached up again, excitement trampling her fear.

The Veil magic parted, and she held it with her mind. She studied the ripple edged arch.

Smaller. It shrunk to half its size without closing.

Intent. It was her intent.

The power of the Veil ripped away from her and slammed the opening closed. She stumbled, felt like someone shoulder checked her and snatched her bag in the same movement.

Okay. She wasn't strong enough to hold it indefinitely.

Maybe with practice?

Ember refocused.

"Child."

Ember flattened her hand against the barrier and pressed without tapping, taking a moment to let the blood rush fade, to allow her frozen thoughts time to thaw, to stop the trembling in her body.

She'd forgotten to check the area.

She hadn't heard anyone coming.

Fae.

She didn't recognize the voice.

What had they seen?

Ember flattened against the solid energy, used it to support her as she turned.

A single Fae with narrow, short locs. Dressed in bright orange and muted brown shades lighter than their mocha-rich eyes. Who held an arrow knocked, pulled, and aimed.

At her.

Oh, verge, what had they seen?

She'd played with opening the barrier. Failed in her attempt to leave Trifecta. In the past, she'd practiced throwing human made things, which would usually be trapped. If she'd brought any for this trip, that call may not have come. The arrow would have been released without warning.

But she hadn't, and the Fae called out. Whatever went through their mind, Ember couldn't guess.

Ember gripped the barrier as if it might give like fabric and allow her to hang on. It didn't, remaining as steady as glass against the length of her spine and the curve of her skull.

"Nicu," the Fae spoke.

Ember swallowed. No question had been asked. She knew she must cooperate, but that did not require volunteering information. A single word could mean anything to the Fae themself, or to the ones hiding in the trees. It did not imply Ember needed to answer.

So she waited, recalling Devi's advice about Fae negotiation five weeks too late. Rule one. Don't enter negotiations whenever possible. Silence proved truly golden.

What was in Ember's favor? The Fae was part of a hunting party, but called no other members forward. The arrow remained in their grip, even though the string was taut.

Chase wasn't able to see her manipulations, which was why she tossed the bag through. Whether Edan saw her throw out Brandt was questionable. If he had, he may not have seen the magic.

Nicu.

Ember only knew that he was different. She didn't know if it was due to him being Fae, or being Nicu.

For now, she'd stay still, keep her hands motionless, her gaze steady, her voice silent.

The string relaxed, the bow lowered, and the Fae spun the arrow until it landed in the quiver. Slow steps backward and they melted into the trees.

Ember closed her eyes, forced herself to count to her breath and breathe to her counts until she reached twenty.

She'd ignored the signs her power wanted to peak when under the Fae's inspection. She locked those thoughts down to keep them from gaining momentum. Ember wasn't sure the Fae left, or if they watched. She took stock, judged the depth and strength of the vibrations within her bones.

The barrier buzzed with her. Blue light filled her vision. A suppressed memory struggled loose. Buried in electricity, buzzing with it instead of burning from it, powerless to stop. Helpless to break free.

With a strangled moan, Ember twisted away from the solid force, stumbled into the trees. The tingling power itched like a million lightning bugs crawled through her body. No Fae stood there to greet her, to challenge her adverse reaction, or shoot with no questions asked. With luck, they continued on their hunt.

Chase's hospitality had never looked better. It was time to get back.

To hide.

To act as if she did not have a Fae guard.

Why did Nicu always have to be right?

It didn't matter. Ember labored forward, waited for the trembling in her legs to subside, then she broke into a run.

Straight into an immovable force that propelled her backward. Ember moved her limbs to scramble away before she hit the ground, her eyes wide and dry, ready to see the point of the arrow headed her way.

The narrow height of the man before her echoed the rise of the surrounding redwoods. His hat shadowed sparkling emerald eyes the same shade as the iridescent vest that showed through his unbuttoned trench coat.

Ember's breath pulsed, tried to keep up with the rapid beat of her heart, building the power within her to a frenzy.

In his hand rested a familiar knife. A thick handle with a curved-tip blade, narrow channels along each side.

Brandt's knife.

Brandt's Wizard.

Blue energy rushed to surround her, to form a barrier between her fear and the knife. The man's gaze shifted to reflect the electric surge of her rogue power. A flush darkened his angled cheekbones. His tongue dampened thin lips. Grasping hands reached for the sparks, spun them together into strings of magic he wrapped around slender fingers as if they were old friends.

The power coated his skin, though he didn't have Nicu's Fae Ink to absorb it. He also lacked Nicu's finesse.

He yanked.

Ember called out, head thrown back as energy ripped through her pores, tearing her body apart from the inside out.

"Goddess!" the man cursed. He opened his trench coat, drew his body over hers and blanketed them both. He wrapped power around them in their own little bubble. Ember gasped against the sharp sparks ricocheting through the trap. Her eyes rolled into the back of her head, and she fell.

11

EMBER

*E*mber turned to her side and inhaled dirt and pine needles. Her arm shook as she lifted, coughing to clear her airways.

"Do you explode often?"

Fades fades fades fades.

She hadn't exposed her power to a complete stranger, had she?

Ember blinked away blurred vision and peeked through her hair to see the man she'd crashed into. He sat amongst the brown and gold leaves, legs crossed and palms flat on his knees. The dirt did not bother him despite his three-piece suit. The bottom buttons of his trench were left open and the excess fabric fell behind him. His hat rested in the hollow of his lap, leaving his wavy auburn hair free to fall against his shoulders.

Why, yes, she had actually exposed her power to a stranger.

Another round of deep hacking cramped Ember's stomach. Her heart pounded at her lungs. She gagged on the convulsions. Tears sprung to her eyes. She squeezed her lashes together to hold them in, strained to swallow.

Ember forced herself into a sitting position and cleared her face with shaking hands. She couldn't afford to keep her back to this stranger who looked like a giant doll, stiff and stuck in his form, features set in a neutral expression.

She also couldn't panic. He hadn't killed her or turned her over to the Fae. He'd shielded her, too, containing the magic which protected her secret. So far, his actions proved friendly, though his intentions were questionable.

He held Brandt's fading knife, which could not be coincidence. This must be the Wizard who wanted to meet her.

Her vision softened, and the world spun clockwise. Ember bent her knees and rested her chin on top of them to settle the dizziness dissolving her awareness. She needed to be in control of herself, or she wouldn't be in control of anything. She clenched her teeth against her tongue, the pain sharpening her senses.

The flat line of the Wizard's mouth angled down, though only at the corners.

"Sparking, then. Has that happened? The shield against your skin?"

He was very observant, marking multiple details from an encounter that had lasted seconds. He gave away some of himself in his questions. Ember was happy to let him do all the talking.

"I see." The man picked up his hat and spun it between long fingers. Head tilted back, he slid the trilby on, hair secured behind his ears and curled against his neck.

Adrenaline cracked in Ember's bones, yet she remained still. This Wizard had cut into Trifecta and tasked Brandt to find her. None of that encouraged trust.

"I understand. Conversation can be difficult with someone you just met. Fine. There was a young man you threw out weeks ago. I'm the one who returned him."

Ember scowled and crossed her arms between her chest and thighs while leveling the Wizard with a glare. At least he brought up Brandt so she didn't have to. Ember tensed, realizing the boy was not in sight. Was he somewhere in the bushes, waiting for his next chance at her?

"Where is he now?" she asked, this question worth breaking her silence.

The man's face faded into neutrality.

"Ah, so you had figured that part out. Very clever." A non-answer focused on her lack of reaction rather than her words. They played a similar game. This was not productive, other than to show he thought her either naïve or stupid.

Ember twisted to all fours before maneuvering to her feet. She'd learned enough. He'd keep her secret for his own reasons, one being he didn't want to interact with Trifecta's mages. So all she had to do was escape to a more populated area.

She chose a random direction. She'd either reach territory she recognized, one of the boundaries of mages, or the barrier. From there, she could head to the Halfer zone and wait until she had a fading Fae guard again.

Ugh. What a horrid thing to look forward to.

The Wizard stood ten feet in front of her in the blink of an eye, in her way. She looked behind her, where he'd been a second ago, then back toward him, mouth parted on a startled gasp.

How had he done that?

"If you've heard about me, you must realize I've been wanting to meet you,' he said. "I would appreciate a few moments of your time. Please."

As if saying 'please' took the sting out of not having a choice.

"You keep interesting company. And you usually have more eyes on you." A warning disguised as an observation. He knew they were alone.

Great.

"What do you want?"

"Do your friends know about your magic?"

"What magic?" Ember asked dryly, without the intention to deceive.

Magic was controllable, something mages harvested and molded into their desires. Witches made gardens grow, healed broken bones with light filtered through a stone. Fae coerced the hidden elegance of an object by bringing its magic to the surface. They also created Ink that could aid magic or bind it, as it bound her.

What she had was chaos ignited. A quirk that let her open the barrier. An echo of the Veil that sometimes coated her skin. A bomb as often as it was helpful.

The man's head tilted askew in a quick, mechanical movement.

"It is difficult to figure out what you know unless you tell me." Oil painted his words. Instead of making him easier to listen to, the slippery inflection sunk a lump of nausea into Ember's gut. "I'm willing to help you.'

Ember slid a foot backward, remembering the greed in his features when he'd stuck his hands into the sparks of her power.

"I will teach you what they won't," he continued.

"And what is that?"

"What you're capable of. To not fear what you are. The pain you felt when I tested the energy within you was an accident. You can learn how to let go, you see, give it rather than have it taken."

Ember flinched at the reminder of his pull. Nicu had never hurt her while engaged with her power.

"I don't want a teacher."

"You've never thought to have one," he countered, and she gasped at the brutal truth of his statement. But then, there'd never been anyone to ask.

"I can show you how your power is meant to be used."

The words sounded more velvet than slick this time. Ember turned her focus from her thoughts to the physical world. The

Wizard had closed the distance while she'd been distracted and was only four feet away.

There was a reason there hadn't been anyone.

She did not practice magic. She was something other than a mage. And she always figured it out on her own. She wasn't going to fall for this dangerous stranger's offer.

"No, thank you." She copied his false civility.

"Is this about trust? I've been here for five weeks. Has any harm come to you or anyone else in my efforts to meet you?"

"Where's Brandt?" she challenged, the question instinctive.

His lips flattened.

"He is engaged in a service that keeps him far from you."

Ember thought she'd be able to breathe if she knew Brandt wasn't a threat. The way the Wizard answered did not inspire that level of relaxation. Did she care if he'd hurt Brandt? Yes, actually. She surprised herself. She wanted Brandt locked up, for him to pay. But she didn't want him to be someone's victim.

The Wizard continued to fill her silences.

"Let's remember, this is about your power, not some simple human. Is it strange to think you have a purpose? That you weren't just a result of random fate?"

"What do you know about my fate?" Ember snapped.

"Perhaps it's worth telling you my name," the man spoke through lips that hardly moved. "I am Tristan."

Ember's knees weakened and she reached blindly, grasping at the brush of bark, using the tree to hold herself up. Words scattered throughout her childhood as her mother tried to explain a man she didn't want to remember.

Stranger. Wizard. Tall and sharp. Slippery snake. Sweet sounding words that tasted like poison.

Disappeared and reappeared without a trace, no warning.

"Ooh. Who is this girl?" A voice like bells danced among the trees. Ember stiffened, not wanting to shift away from Tristan despite the intruder. The Wizard pulled the knife from the interior of his coat. Goosebumps speckled Ember's skin at the defensive action.

"Not the time, Charlah," Tristan sneered.

From between the trees, a barefoot girl drifted until she stood inches in front of Ember, ignoring Tristan and his weapon. Long iridescent hair fell in straight lines over a belted green slip dress that did nothing to protect against the cold. A spherical clear quartz dangled from a hemp necklace, the weave matching the thicker twists of her black and yellow beaded belt.

Light, neutral colors vanished in the absorbent darkness of her eyes. Ember sunk into the obscurity, gasping when specks of light shifted, as if miniature galaxies moved within.

The girl's pink lips curled over white teeth. She leaned forward with the eagerness of a child picking a honeyed sweet.

"Hello," she chimed.

"Time to go," Tristan ordered.

"I do not agree." A ragged nail approached Ember's cheek. Ember reached for her power, tried to actively create a barrier between her and the oncoming touch. The pinpoint lights in Charlah's eyes flared, and she pulled back slightly, brow wrinkled.

"A shame." Tristan's voice passed over Charlah's head, his appearance sudden, the knife raised over the newcomer's shoulder.

The girl disappeared, leaving Tristan pointing the blade at Ember. Blue energy shimmered into a shield, and she stumbled back.

Charlah's figure blurred behind Tristan, then solidified for her attack. The Wizard turned in time to duck the clawed hand she reached toward his cheek, then was gone before he straightened. The space in front of Ember emptied, and Tristan stood ten yards away where the girl wrenched her arm from his grip.

Ember's eyes teared from the strain of trying to detect the

pair as they used the same strange speed. They appeared and disappeared, moving as if distance didn't matter, pausing only in attack. Charlah scratched with clawed fingers, intent on harm. The man swung the knife, though in careful strokes meant for gentle wounds. He favored attempts to catch the girl over injuring her, giving him a disadvantage.

A headache split the space between Ember's eyes. Keeping track was impossible. There was an equal chance of running into them or away from them. She hoped they would take their fight elsewhere, forget her altogether so she could risk escape.

The girl hummed, reigned in her attacks in favor of stealing the weapon that threatened her. She positioned herself behind Tristan. She scratched at his eyes and he swung toward her. Charlah anticipated the Wizard's movement, appeared on his opposite side and gripped just below the blade.

Tristan's tactics changed in an instant. He held firm to the hilt, tucked his arm against his body, bringing Charlah with him. He wrapped his free hand around her wrist. Eyes sparkled with intended cruelty and he squeezed flesh into bone.

Charlah whimpered, and she pressed against Tristan's chest.

"I'm letting go!" She supported her statement with fingers open and flared.

Tristan released her. "I told you. It is time."

Her pink lips coiled.

"And I said no."

Charlah slammed into the Wizard. He grit his teeth, kept himself from moving more than two steps. He tried to reach her with one hand, the other wrapped around the knife he refused to give up. Charlah grasped the blade, the sharp curve nestled into the flesh of her palm. Tristan's white knuckle grip strained apart as she slipped the handle out of his fist. Charlah took possession of the hilt and opened her grasp on the blade, skin solid and whole.

The Wizard lunged to retrieve his prize. Charlah disappeared. Tristan followed.

Ember was alone, but her head was on fire. She gave in to the weakness in her legs and lowered her quaking body to the ground. Memories burned as she relived the moments where Susan truly lost control. The pain of her mother's past shattered Ember's present too many times to count.

Another memory scorched Ember. Susan screaming at Ember after Nicu freed her from the barrier. *"You chose him, I see. You chose magic."*

Ember had thought her mom meant she chose Nicu. She'd been wrong.

Susan meant the Wizard who was Ember's father. Somehow, she'd known Tristan was back, and that he wanted Ember. No, not her. The power inside her.

But for what?

12

DEVI

"Mom." Devi's jaw ached with the effort to speak without clenching her teeth. "I do not have time for this."

"Then make it," Leona snapped. "The more we offer Trifecta, the better footing we have as a coven. If you can teach others how to refine the waste oil into lubricants for the humans' solar and electric machines, that's one more mark in our favor."

"Love potions and plague cures didn't keep our ancestors from being burned at the stake."

"Devi!" Leona stopped, drawing the slow pace Devi forced them on to a halt. She pressed her hand against her forehead and pushed back frizzy, carrot-red hair, damp despite the chill. Her fingerless gloves matched the bright, leaf-pattern fabric of her quilted coat, camouflage for when she entered her greenhouse, but garish against the grey, naked outer walls of the warehouses.

"Look. Think of this as one of those puzzles you love. Every piece needs to be available to complete the picture. Right now, we don't have enough pieces to secure our place in Terra. These services we offer provide leverage to keep us at the table, to buy time to find them. For that, we have to remain essential. Can you please do your part? For the coven?"

This would be the second time her mother had asked her to do something specific for the coven. The last request to investigate an unknown spell had led Devi to an electric storm at the End of the World, a lost knife she desperately wanted, and left her with a prisoner who disappeared a few hours later. In other words, it had not gone well. Devi narrowed her eyes.

"My skills are better spent elsewhere."

"Where, Devi? Finding a human boy with no trace of magic in his veins? Locating a Wizard able to hide his tracks, who takes our hidden messages asking for a meeting without returning them?"

Not hardly.

Devi wanted to discover how Nicu and Ember's Ink connected to the barrier, and solve the mystery of the missing knife.

Telling her mother the truth was tempting. Explain Brandt had attacked the Trimarked Child with the spelled blade, somehow causing Ember to merge with the Veil energy. Yet, she did not speak the words. Devi doubted it would result in the action she desired, and it would open an inquiry that could stop Devi's progress for far longer than a morning class on waste oil refinement.

"At the very least, we should guard against the possibility of Brandt's return to the humans," Devi charged. "Isn't that what's behind this urgency to belong? Their whispers over the runaways that might cause trouble for us?"

Leona flushed a red in contrast to her hair.

"Do not assume you know all just because you were born in this realm and I was not. Brandt's possible return is nothing we can take action against without betraying that we played a part by holding him for his crimes. If he finds a way, we will talk about our strategy. The Fae have softened the lines of distrust so we have the opportunity to find our peaceful place. It can benefit us if we use it well."

"The Fae magic may break, or wear down."

"Which is why we take advantage of every opportunity." Leona squared her shoulders on a sharp inhale. "I have asked you as your mother for weeks. Now I am going to order you as the High Priestess. Teach."

Devi worked to unclench her jaw and closed her eyes to guard against the glare she wanted to send her mother's way. She did not have the same strength of belief in the Fae's spell. Leona had not seen Brandt break, no longer placated by the spirit magic. If one human wiggled free, why not the rest? Unfettered humans discovering mages imprisoned one of their own, no matter the reason, would be easy fuel for conflict.

Footsteps bounced along the broken paths. Devi and her mother had gone deep enough into the industrial zone that restoration efforts had stopped at peeling back the black asphalt and piling the chunks against the sides of nearby buildings. They turned to greet the young, light-footed runner, surprised to find he was followed by Aaron and his bouncing stride.

Leona's eyes softened, a smile curled her painted lips, and the creases in her skin shifted from across her forehead to beside her eyes. Her hands fluttered as if she expected their guest to take them in greeting.

"If it isn't my favorite friend-seeker," she purred. "How have you been?"

Aaron's steps hesitated with the welcome. His eyes flickered between Devi and her mother with a slight thinning of his lips.

"Better."

Devi marked his flat tone. This was not puppy dog Aaron. What dampened his spirits?

"Have you come for another charm? Perhaps with a bit

more trust included this time?" Leona drifted, gesturing for Aaron to take her arm. He stepped to the side with a half smile.

"No, thank you. I'm not sure the last one worked, anyway."

"Oh? You didn't end up with a new friend?"

Aaron shook his head, then stopped in thought.

"Well, maybe. But I hadn't asked for—"

"Sometimes what we need is not what we're asking for." Leona attempted to take Aaron's arm again.

"Do you think you could scry this time? Try to look for my f-friend?"

Leona's hands drifted in exaggerated motions until they linked together in rest. The messenger gasped at Aaron's question, drawing the human's attention for a moment. Leona shook her head with a generous sigh, as if she regretted the refusal.

"No, I'm sorry. My magic cannot help you in the way you wish."

Devi snapped her mint-gem eyes to her mother's face, trying to see past the Harmless Woman façade she put on for Aaron's sake. Of course Devi assumed Leona scried for Brandt, had presumed she hadn't been able to find him as she hadn't found the Wizard. Her refusal wasn't about how magic couldn't help, but how Aaron wouldn't like the answer.

What did the High Priestess know that she wasn't sharing? What had she seen when she looked for the lost human? Alerted by her mother's particular phrasing, Devi doubted the request came simply to enforce their place in Trifecta. Was it related to why Leona was desperate for Devi to teach, a task that required her to be deep within the Circle, surrounded by Witches and Wizards?

"In that case, I need Devi," Aaron said.

Devi's attention spread between them once more. If her mother hadn't shared her worrying thoughts yet, she wouldn't say now, but Devi would remain alert for hints.

"Oh. May I ask why?" Leona's octave raised to a near squeak.

Aaron glanced at Devi and his hands dove into his jeans' hip pockets, elbows compressing the sides of his navy puffer coat, a sign he wasn't sure how to proceed. Aaron had helped Devi bring Brandt onto Witch land, but Leona wasn't aware. Her mother knew Devi investigated a mysterious trail through the forest, then returned with a human who had worked with the invading Wizard. Aaron wouldn't know which pieces Devi shared. His ability to exercise caution impressed.

How quickly the human became acclimated with mages, and the web was difficult to emerge from. He would be an ally they must watch, never fully certain of his loyalties. Devi would have to remind Chase of that the next time they met for magic lessons.

"It's just... You see, I..." Aaron stumbled with his explanation.

"He's been watching the Lee's house for me," Devi composed before the confusion in Leona's eyes shifted to suspicion, careful to keep vicious satisfaction from sharpening the edges of her smile. "It turns out he only lives a few doors down from Susan. To return your favor of the charm, he was happy to help."

"Right," he agreed, the word drawn in a line of caution. The hesitation in his eyes was heavy enough to give away their secret, but Leona wasn't paying attention. Her focus seemed to turn to the mental calculations likely playing out in her head, her hands in a white knuckle grip.

Interesting. Was she hiding her anger or something else? Despite the random shiver, Leona's facial expression didn't break.

"Any particular reason the house should be watched?" Leona asked in a tip-toe-voice.

"Because it's helpful," Devi snapped, then buried her irritation under a deep breath. "It has to do with the person who made that trail you found," she continued through her teeth, hoping her balancing act wouldn't land her in the mud.

Leona's smile grew even though her skin paled, her persona fighting against her true reaction. Aaron stared at his toes as he bounced on them.

"Yeah, the thing is." Aaron dropped to his heels and raised his chin with sudden determination. "Someone was in the forest today. I didn't see them approach, or anything, but you said to tell you."

"Exactly," Devi interrupted before he got too carried away. "Can you show me where?"

Irritation snapped Leona back toward her mother self, and away from the personality she showed to humans. "You are supposed to be teaching right now."

Devi blew out a hot breath and crossed her arms to hide clenched fists. Leona was not making this easy.

"Teaching?" Aaron's brow furrowed. "Like, how to track?"

"How to clean waste oil." Leona's eyes brightened with the return of the Harmless Woman, her hands free to dance with her words. "Isn't it amazing? Devi discovered a way to separate the molecules into lubricants."

"Wait." Aaron paced away a few small steps, then returned to them in two long strides. "You are trying to clean something while the humans are—" Aaron grunted to a stop, his cheeks drawn. "Devi, I really need to talk to you."

"My High Priestess has asked me to stay."

Aaron's lips vibrated against words he withheld, his eyes hot blue coals.

Devi closed her eyes on a long breath, opened them at the same pace. This level of fury had one likely source. Nicu had told him Brandt was gone.

Leona had miscalculated.

"Mom."

Aaron's strangled growl bounced off the fractured stone pieces that surrounded them. The strength of his steps echoed the heat of his anger. Devi blinked at his retreating form.

"It has to be something more." Devi hoped her words sunk in while her mother stared after the human.

"Obviously." Leona's lips thinned. "Are your notes complete?"

Devi thought back to her scattered remarks for the oil project, transcribed into a single notebook as she completed her experiments, in part to combine the knowledge. In part, to hide her research into Fae Ink.

"Yes. The green cover. It's labeled."

"Very well." Leona's nose flared as she breathed deep. "Go after him."

Devi did not like to run. The gems in her layered bracelets banged against each other over the tight sleeves of her fitted goldenrod sweater. Wind tangled the curls of her cranberry hair, and her russet orange skirt threatened to hobble her legs.

She bolted before whatever internal battle Leona fought shifted out of Devi's favor. She rushed to catch up with the human, because she'd seen what one of those angry creatures could do five weeks prior and was desperate to defuse the situation. Thankfully, she caught up with Aaron before he left the inner Circle.

He glanced sideways at her but remained silent as the pair passed the rubble of abandoned storage warehouses. They passed into the outer, reclaimed portion of the Circle. The coven renovated the old factories into apartments, work spaces, and school rooms, then planted vines to envelop the gloomy exterior with living beauty. Curved pathways encouraged wandering steps through gardens laced between buildings so one could enjoy the flowers and berries that bloomed year round, thanks to magic s touch.

"Not much progress with the rebuilding efforts." Aaron's judgement was sharp, a passive aggressive response.

She could accept passive.

"It takes time to heal the earth and remove impurities. We focus on healing the land before it's cultivated or decorated."

Aaron grunted, his scowl locked in place. There had been an apology in Devi's words, mentioning how some progress must be slow despite frustration. She'd warned against drawing conclusions about the surface without knowing what was being done underneath.

Aaron understood none of that, and it was not in her to expand on the sentiment.

"Your mom is the High Priestess."

Ah, he got that part.

"Yes. And I have been avoiding this teaching task for weeks. Like you, I recognize there are more important matters." She refrained from mentioning that important meant different things to them, not when their goals aligned at the moment.

Aaron blew a harsh breath through pursed lips. He rolled his shoulders into a more relaxed line and put his hands in his pockets.

"Parents can be tough. I'm here because of my dad."

Devi waited for him to say more. They continued across the cultivated gravel at the edge of the Circle until it blended with the harshness of a broken road abandoned by the humans. At this in between, where the trees stood tall and the Halfer zone was yet to be seen, Aaron slowed to a halt.

"Why isn't anyone looking for Brandt?"

"Of course we are." Devi bit her tongue, sharp teeth to stop her sharp tone. "We have searched. We have placed spells to alert us to movement, left messages asking the rogue to make contact."

"Why only tell us now?"

Devi licked her lips when she wanted to scowl. Aaron clearly considered himself part of some group now. Great. Except, there was no group. She hadn't told an 'us.' She had only told Nicu. The Fae's indiscretion came as a surprise to

Devi, and she added the why of it to her ever growing list of unanswered questions.

"This intruder is a Wizard. The High Priestess prefers we settle this within our own bubble. I don't always agree with my mother. Given the delicacy of the matter, I thought it wouldn't hurt to alert the person closest to Ember." Devi meant Nicu, of course. Let Aaron take from her words whatever he wanted.

Aaron nodded, tilted his head toward the canopy.

"Well, you might get more than expected. My dad is worried Brandt committed suicide." Each word fell out of Aaron's mouth like teeth pulled against his will. "He wants me to see if I can find the Underground. If I can't give him an answer or produce Brandt, he's likely to go looking for himself."

"Did you warn Chase?"

"He's disappeared. The Halfers aren't telling me where. I came here since you meet up with him sometimes." Aaron shrugged and brought his gaze level.

What was it with Nicu and Chase sharing insider knowledge with this human? How had they not considered the possibility of a similar break in him as had happened with Brandt? Devi captured frustrated air within her lungs, not wanting to distract Aaron from his speech.

"The thing is, it's more complicated than that. My dad isn't the only one looking. The humans are worried about the runaways, and they're asking me a lot of questions because of Brandt. They think since we were such close friends, I must know where he is. Where to find the Underground."

Devi's chest rose and fell with quick breaths, his words an echo of what she'd told her mother. She'd meant it as an excuse. Aaron saw deeper into it. Devi's anxiety expanded beyond the fear of one boy breaking free of Fae compulsion, to all of the humans. Investigating the Halfers was a gateway to inspecting mages.

Fear beat at her logic, screamed the Fae spell must be

fading. Facts didn't support that theory and she refused the false narrative by focusing on the questions.

Why, oh why, would humans suddenly focus on something they'd ignored for decades? What had encouraged them to start an investigation that would guarantee conflict between races?

A consciousness so recent, in fact, so against the norm, so soon after Trifecta had been infiltrated.

"What else?" Aaron murmured. "Um, the people at today's market were acting weird because of a pregnant runaway. Oh, and some guy showed up at the house asking about his lost sister."

Devi zeroed in on Aaron, his words connecting with her thoughts.

"What guy?"

Aaron's brow wrinkled. "You know, it's hard. I didn't remember that happened until I said it. Dad had him at the door. I don't think he came in? Right?"

He asked, as if she might have the answers. As if his active memory did not match his instinctive one.

Magic.

Finally, something easy.

Devi's touch danced over her bracelets. Opal, pyrite, hematoid, blue chalcedony, and aurora quartz. She spun them in her palm, fingers open so light filled the microscopic crystal formations of each gem.

"Kneel."

Aaron's face went slack with shock. "Wh-what do you want?"

"Kneel." This time power flowed through her voice as she began the Work within her mind, a spell to remove the fog and reclaim genuine memories. Aaron eased to one knee, then the other. Devi cupped his forehead in the palm of her empty hand, increased volume, and closed her eyes to free what Aaron had been encouraged to forget.

13

NICU

A whistle cut through the trees, low as the wind, insistent as a storm.

Nicu and Branna paused their light jog through the western forest of Trifecta. They had been searching in a grid pattern most of the morning, focusing on these deep, animal inhabited lands as the most likely place to find hidden people. Their efforts proved fruitless. The few abandoned campfire rings were of human use from summer days, too old to have hosted Brandt or the mysterious Wizard. Nor had they discovered any odd placement of magic for Nicu to trace.

The patrol who signaled them was the third set of Fae Nicu and Branna had encountered. Usually, fewer hunting parties shared the forest. In fact, few of them were true hunters. After the Wizard had cut his way into Trifecta, Elder Neyu had increased the Fae presence. They were disguised as a precaution against accusations of breaking the Laws of Convergence that preserved the peace between races.

The five Fae eased from the forest, hidden until they chose to be seen. They'd been well camouflaged despite the garish orange tunics the humans insisted hunting parties wore. A useless request. Fae were adept at keeping out of sight with or without the bright clothing.

Each Fae carried a long knife at their belt, a bow, and a quiver filled with artisan arrows as deadly as they were beautiful. A true hunting party, then, and not one of the decoys.

"Nicu," the patrol leader greeted. "I am Altaya." Mocha-rich eyes betrayed a moment of unease that they quickly tucked away.

"We are searching for signs of recent human activity." Nicu's announcement rippled through the Fae as their wariness at seeing the Trimarked Child's guardian eased.

"The Child is waiting for you."

A statement of fact, not a question. One Nicu had not been prepared for. He kept his reaction within his mind, his only movement a sharp dip of his chin.

"She didn't say you were near," Altaya continued.

Fades. The hybrid girl could not follow instruction, could not remain unseen.

"She would not," Nicu agreed, his voice light, as if Ember followed his orders.

Branna hummed a note so softly it only drifted into his ears. A deer burst into their space. Startled to find them, the animal spun and leapt back into the trees. Four of the Fae turned their heads to watch its flight. Altaya regarded Nicu.

Branna's warning would not have been about the creature. He needed the hunting party gone.

"Have a successful hunt," Nicu bid them farewell.

Altaya twitched their fingers. The team drifted away at the signal. They were the last to leave, trailing the other four. Nicu watched the group follow the deer's path, enforcing a steady breath on his lungs.

"The spirits are agitated," Branna announced when it was safe. Her eyes softened in focus, her hands floated in the air at her sides. The scythe-shaped lines of her tattoos flared and thickened, reminiscent of a bird spreading its feathers.

To access the High Magic of spirit was forbidden for every Terra-bound Fae, except for the necromancer. Branna's paranormal abilities meant she did not have to reach into the soul realm to speak to the spirits. A part of her existed there, tied to both life and death. Her story was horrific and exceptional. The Fae did not approve, but they were not fools. Offending death was never wise.

Branna's curved hands slowly twisted toward the sky, cupping the energy of the spirit. Tattoos one shade darker than her skin slid over veins and muscle, shifted over the folds in her palms.

A line of grey between the tones caught Nicu's attention as he waited for Branna to complete her communion. He focused on the anomaly. A lighter, ashen shadow rested within the creases of movement.

Distinct and precise, not a sign of dryness. Her fluid motions discarded the idea she might be in pain. A change, nonetheless, and one he had not heard of as a Fae affliction.

Wist's warning from this morning intruded. Could this be from the Trimark medallion?

Yet, this change was of her skin, not her soul. The Elder's motives were circumspect. Discomfort settled at the base of Nicu's spine.

Branna's Ink relaxed, rested within her pores. Nicu did not miss how they remained stretched into her palms.

"Your tattoos have shifted."

"As they do when I exercise my power." Her harsh tone eased his concern, yet caution did not vacate his mind.

"Branna." Nicu would not ask her how she felt. Wist's words would not be shared without more evidence. He could only let her know he had noticed.

"Should we talk about tattoos acting oddly?" she demanded. "How did you get yours to leave your body when you rescued the Child? It was as if the infamous Shade had arrived in Terra."

One of the powerful Fae still residing in Gypsum, Shade was the only known Fae to wield her tattoo as a physical weapon. Legend spoke of her as an outlaw, dabbling with powers the Fae should not use. It was magic Nicu never had the chance or desire to study. That he'd pushed Ink from his pores and used it as a physical force without training or intent set him apart once again.

If he pushed Branna about her tattoos, she would fight back with more deflections. He would not bring up Wist's visits, or his warnings about her changing to the point of no longer being Fae, which left him without leverage. As Branna did not appear to mind the marks on her skin, he let her keep her secrets. But he would watch, be on guard to not only make certain she was okay, but discern whether there was any truth in Wist's twisted warning.

"What have you learned?" he asked, dropping his inquiry. The change of topic suited Branna, who stretched her neck to ease its tension.

"Something bright in the forest unnerves the spirits, but does not scare them. A sunshine soul. I am not certain of their meaning."

"Should the living worry?" Nicu asked.

"It is unclear. They can only confirm this is not Brandt or his Wizard, and that the soul arrived today, from outside Trifecta."

Nicu's spine locked into place.

The one day he had not patrolled the border, where he abandoned his duty in favor of this unproductive search.

"Did they cut through?" His quiet question drew Branna's deep mauve eyes into contact with his.

"You did not feel it."

A good argument. Nicu suspected the new entry was of a different sort. How could someone else get in, then? Where else? What place might he not notice passage?

"Nicu," Branna gasped, turning to shield her face. "It is her! She is the sunshine soul."

Power jetted past him, Witch in nature, strong in form. His eyes narrowed on the unexpected flow. It had a skin of its own, hiding whatever moved inside.

"Get ready," he warned Branna.

Nicu flexed his fingers and called forth his Ink. He brushed the stream, tasted its form with his tattoos. His hand punched into the power, wrapped around the top of an arm, and pulled out who he hoped was the Wizard.

He did not expect a woman with blinding white hair and shimmering onyx eyes.

His surprise did not affect his choices. Nicu kept hold of the strange Witch. The woman did not fight him. Instead, she raised a blade made of starfall iron. Nicu recognized the curve at its tip and the sharp, narrow channels on either side.

He shifted his grip from her bicep to the wrist holding the weapon, drew it against his ribs, knowing a close weapon to be safer than one that swung.

"How did you find this knife?" he asked, hoping the answer might lead him to the Wizard.

The woman's pink lips pursed toward him and she tugged to test the strength of his grasp.

"You don't ask interesting questions."

"Why are you so bright?" Branna demanded.

The woman grinned. Her midnight eyes widened, displaying specks of distant light.

"What a lovely question. How do you see my color?" She leaned around Nicu to find Branna. Her smile transformed into a silent scream. She jerked away, cheeks flush with accusation.

"You tricked me!' she screamed. "She cannot have me! I will not allow her to tear my souls apart!"

The woman struck Nicu with more strength than he'd expected from her slight build. He kept her weapon hand close while he blocked her jabs at his stomach, ribs, and face. Enraged he hadn't let go, she shifted the knife and sliced it across his left bicep.

Injured nerves loosened Nicu's grip. The Witch disappeared, her magic trail dissipating in her wake.

"She is gone," he announced to Branna, who removed her hands from her face.

"What happened? She blinded me." Branna blinked away the last bright spots that filtered her vision, gasped at the blood that seeped into Nicu's grey coat despite the pressure he placed with his opposite hand.

"It is not deep," he assured her. "The woman panicked. A quick attack for a sure escape. She used the knife Devi has claimed, one we thought the Wizard held."

"How is this possible? Do you know what she is?"

"An anomaly, but not like us." Nicu bent his arm to steady the wound. "More similar to Shade, specific and powerful in her skills, if that path is an indication."

"Great." Branna's lips twisted. "What now? I cannot give you the magic you need to fix that."

"I will tend to it myself," Nicu responded. He did not want to draw attention to his evasion of duty.

As if his words of self-healing had called to it, a whisper of blue-tinted power flavored the air. Branna frowned and studied the space between the trees.

"The spirits are reflecting Veil energy like it is dust in the air. Is the barrier shedding again?" she asked, referring to when they'd discovered Veil fragments scattered in the Lee's lawn five weeks ago. He'd been investigating the anomaly just before he'd seen the hybrid girl spark with his own eyes.

"It was never the barrier," Nicu murmured, able to see the specks without the help of spirits. Branna's scowl demanded an answer. He raised a brow in reply. "You are the one who found the concentration around the Trimarked Child's home, there when we discovered she has a unique connection to this energy."

The fragments hadn't come from the Veil, but the hybrid girl. Branna may have learned the truth already, had she spoken to him in the last few weeks.

Branna's cheeks colored as she put the pieces together, though not in embarrassment.

"Forgive me if I'm more concerned about a lost Fae than the wayward Child," she hissed.

"Edan will endure both our displeasure at the pain he's caused you."

Branna's body jerked in a small step back, and a strangled sound escaped her throat. Nicu ignored her reaction out of respect as he studied the surrounding power.

The sky was not dark. There was no threat of a storm. Yet, the remnants of Ember's morning lapse behind the Halfer Zone circled. Nicu activated his tattoos, let the magic saturated air settle, absorb into his Ink.

The particles seeped into his body, eased into the aches caused by his fight with the strange woman with a sunshine soul. The laceration stitched together, as if a part of his healing spell had broken off and floated along until, by chance, it had found his wounds on the breeze.

Chance had nothing to do with this. Fate would be the hand guiding this one.

Nicu's fingers twitched, and he stopped himself from reaching for the pendant hidden beneath the heavy fall of braids at his neck.

The Fae had a complicated relationship with fate. Fate created the path. Chaos used any means to enforce that path. The Fae were only comfortable when they wove their own passage through the dictates of fate.

Nicu had enticed chaos and had brought its attention when he manipulated the Trimarked talisman. He would not be forgiven for the trespass. A High Magic thread interlaced the healing energy, subtle and sharp. One that explained how this morning's magic found its way to him at this exact moment.

Wish Magic. An echo of a wish that would be made in the future for Ember that meant he needed to be whole in body. Therefore, fate made it so. Who or when the wish would come, Nicu would not know until the moment arrived. But this magic made it a certainty. Almost.

Nicu turned from Branna. Emptied his lungs, then filled them to capacity.

Wish Magic was the reason the Fae banned the manipulation of Space and Time energies. Working with these energies and engaging in High Magic risked more than the wrath of the Fae. The universe owned his consequences, and never played nice with the one who dared to change the fabric of reality.

Though he could not see the path chaos forced him to, he knew it was not the direction he'd chosen. The one of balance between the Fae and Ember.

The wish had not been asked, or granted, yet. There was an opportunity to reverse the decision. He would use his Fae discipline to deny the wish, create his own passage. His wound would reopen when he refused. His body would break under the force of fate. The price far less than what the universe would claim.

If his control was not enough, if the choice was taken from him, only one truth would matter.

The Fae must never know.

14

EMBER

*E*mber rested against a split boulder, one flat side a seat, the other an oddly angled backrest. The day was cold, the stone colder, yet movement was impossible. The confusion in her mind was thick and heavy, holding every brain cell hostage.

Even if she could think, she couldn't solve this puzzle.

She needed more information.

She didn't want to learn.

Ember leaned her head back, her face parallel with the sky. Her soul crystalized as dark and grey as the stone. How long would she have to sit here before her heart turned just as cold?

"Hello," a voice chimed.

Ember jerked. The involuntary movement tested her balance on the edge of the boulder, and she counteracted the fall with her hands flung out. She faced the girl looking down at her, noted the soft smile on pink lips and dug her fingers into her thighs to keep from screaming.

She had never seen a bear in this forest. Others had encountered mountain lions. Not her. She imagined if she ever did, that fear would not equal what she encountered staring into the black abyss that replaced Charlah's eyes.

"What are you?" Ember's voice wavered.

"Clever girl, to ask what, not who. I have the same question as you. Should we swap stories?"

Ember whipped her head around to search between the trees, wondering if Tristan was near.

"If you're looking for that frivolous earth-mage, he ran away when I found the fate-mages. Which was perfect, because it meant I could come find you again."

"Why?" The word exploded from Ember's chest. Charlah's cheerful innocence wasn't to be trusted. Her impossible eyes told Ember all she needed to know.

This girl hid her danger well.

Charlah perched on the edge of the boulder, crowding Ember to the opposite side. She placed the wicked point of the blade against the surface and spun it with one hand.

"Tristan brought me here to help feed his tree, but I said no. You are very strong, too, but he didn't ask you. I want to learn why."

Ember's thoughts tangled around Charlah's remarks, not able to sort them out.

"Feed a tree?"

"Yep. Because of what I am."

"What are you?" Ember mumbled the question, uncertain she wanted the answer.

"I am a Queen, of course."

Ember took in the ragged nails, unadorned hair, and simple dress.

"Your Majesty?" Ember asked, wondering if she was being polite or complicit in this woman's self-delusion. Brilliant jewel-toned laughter filled the air at a pitch that could break glass.

"Not that kind. My type of Queen doesn't exist in Terra. Well, not until I came, of course. My soul is too big for one body, and that makes me a Queen." The black orbs of her eyes lifted from the blade to Ember, savage shadows surrounded by ethereal hair. "It's my turn now. What are you, my dear, little thing?"

The Queen leaned in until she was inches away from Ember, her parted lips and flushed cheeks betraying her eager interest in the answer. Her proximity brought an instant, dewy sweat to Ember's brow that simultaneously froze in the chill breeze. She tried to speak, but her dry throat seized and Ember had to force a cough before her voice surged back to life.

"Trimarked."

The girl shook her head. She shifted to tuck the knife into her belt, freeing her hands to pull herself further onto the boulder.

"No, no, no. That's what they did to you because of what you are. Tricky fate-mages." Charlah eased in, smelling of honey and dust, her smile open, her black eyes pools of curiosity.

Ember would have to disappoint. "They didn't tell me."

"I guess we'll have to find out together." Charlah sounded like they were about to play her favorite game. She even clapped her hands. Ember fixated on the sharp, zigzag points of her long nails.

Then those broken edges reached for Ember's cheek. The Queen's other fingers cradled the quartz resting above her heart. Ember leaned away, flinched in preparation for the contact.

"Oooh, this is pretty," Charlah muttered. A ripple of light-blue had blocked her touch.

Ember breathed deep to capture her sigh, not wanting the sound to alert the Queen to her relief. Her mind had frozen, her intent non-existent. She hadn't willed the magic forward, but it came anyway in automatic defense.

"It's Veil energy! How did you get it?" Glossy eyes widened and reflected a sapphire glow.

Ember's chest heaved with phantom breaths even as her airways clenched shut.

"So, you were an experiment!"

An expulsion of air rocked Ember's core. "What?"

"For me, they made twins and twins and twins inside one belly until there were ten. While the cells were still new, they combined them so only one body was born. They wanted to make a goddess. Instead, they got a Queen."

Ember had never been called an experiment before. She realized that's exactly what she was. Her mother, a human woman, tricked into becoming pregnant with a Wizard's child. Then Susan was forced onto Fae land to give birth.

But why? Ember remembered the greed in Tristan's face when he'd seen her power. He definitely wanted it, but had offered to teach her how to command it.

"What does it mean?" Ember whispered.

"You fascinate me," the Queen spoke with laughter in her words. "Who cares what it means. What can you do with this power? Just make shields? Ooh, can you turn invisible, like the Veil itself?"

"I can't control it." Truth without story, following her gut that honesty was the way to go.

Charlah's laugh rang through the tree boughs.

"What is control? I don't control what I do. That doesn't mean we can't use it."

"Use it without control?" Ember asked. What would Nicu say about that?

"Sure. It's there anyway. Direct it, bend it, so it doesn't use you, first."

Well, fades. That made a certain kind of sense.

Charlah squared herself toward Ember, her eyes bright and her smile taking up most of her face.

"I bet you can even break through the Veil for me, and I wouldn't need this knife! The spell is nearly done, anyhow. But I'd need to collect my family, of course."

Ember's vision darkened while the girl crowding her rambled. Charlah had guessed her ability by observing the passive power Ember's body created. She sounded simple, but as her eyes proved, the Queen was much more than Ember could handle.

"Branna."

Nicu's voice burst through Ember. She twisted toward the sound. The sinister shade of a tree angled before him, between where he stood and the boulder where Charlah sat with her.

Branna opened the center of the shadow, peeled it away like a cloak. She stepped out, a dark phantom that invoked thoughts of death. A midnight halo increased the size of her presence as she invaded the daylight.

Ember pressed herself into the upright half of the boulder, trying to find a crack big enough to hide from the power the necromancer generated.

Charlah's scream cut through it all, her full black eyes dwarfed by the darkness that was Branna.

"I will get a family and I will stop you!" Charlah threatened, the edges of her shriek grinding into a growl. Her gaze flickered toward Ember, then she was gone.

Branna released the shadows back to nature with Charlah's disappearance. Nicu approached Ember. A dark stain on his left arm drew her attention in the moment before he spoke.

"Did she harm you?" Nicu asked.

"Perhaps you should ask a different question," Branna snapped. "They looked very cozy together."

Ember's mouth gaped toward the female Fae. The attitude was one she remembered, one she'd sparred against before. But the shadows were new, and Ember trembled, fear a clammy casing on her tongue.

The way Nicu's eyes lingered on Branna a few extra seconds suggested the necromancer had surprised him as well. Not a comforting thought.

Ember cleared her throat, focused on Branna's words and

not her show of power. She wasn't sure what to tell them. That the Queen was interested in Ember's connection to the barrier energy? How she ran into Tristan and discovered he was her father?

Have them lock her in Chase's house and remove even more of her freedoms?

"I don't really know," Ember settled on an answer. "She said something about finding a family, but she didn't make much sense."

Nicu studied Ember's features, looking for hidden notes in her answer. Ember shifted between her sitting bones, then scrambled to her feet, wishing she looked more composed than a frightened rabbit.

"Why are you out here? Where is Chase?" Nicu asked, allowing her slight evasion for now.

"How should I know?" Ember grumbled, and wished her tongue worked well enough to snap back at him. Regain some normalcy in her life.

"Then he is most likely unharmed," Nicu concluded. Guilt flushed through Ember, then flashed into reflexive anger that had little to do with his question and everything to do with the chaos of the day.

"Scared you lost your pet?" Ember words sprung from the irritation she felt toward Chase and the relationships with Nicu and Aaron that he'd hid from her.

"You cannot tame a wild animal," Nicu countered.

Explosive laughter singed Ember's throat as her emotions ricocheted. Her body couldn't decide. Should she be enraged, relieved, or frightened? There was no option to turn it off, to feel nothing. So she laughed, doubled over against the pain of not having a choice. She caught her breath after a moment, focused on the Fae watching her as if she'd lost her mind.

"If he's a wild animal, then what am I?" Ember demanded.

Nicu's eyes softened in opposition to his tight frown, as if he had thoughts that warred with each other. He turned to Branna without answering.

"Can you follow her again?"

Branna nodded, though her eyes stuck to Ember. "What are we going to do with her?"

"Since her human guard proved fallible, she will stay with us."

As Ember thought, less freedom. At least she had company. Solitude had led to more than its share of problems today.

"She will slow us down," Branna argued.

Nicu's body rippled from alert to commanding.

"There are too many variables moving," he countered. "Three beings are interested in the Trimarked Child for unknown reasons." Nicu refocused on Ember. "She is a challenge on her own."

"Exactly. How are we to focus on the sunshine soul with her distraction?"

"Branna." Nicu's warning deepened in his chest, a tone Ember had become familiar with over the years. "Start trailing the stranger."

The black-clad Fae glared the last of her disagreement at Nicu, and sent a curled lip toward Ember. Dismissing them both, Branna turned to her task, calling forth shadows to protect her vision as she searched for sunshine amid the trees.

Nicu gestured for Ember to fall behind Branna's lead, then he took the rear, leaving enough room for Ember to pass without contact. She flinched when she remembered how the touch of his skin had sent his thoughts into her mind. Nicu's amber eyes burned with the same memory, along with a command that did not leave his lips, yet she understood it as clearly as if his words had slipped into her mind again.

Do not make him touch her.

15

EMBER

*E*mber's thighs burned with each demanding step. She hadn't had breakfast before her morning of exertion, and the lack of fuel took its toll. She stumbled and Nicu's sudden heat at her side inspired her to regain her balance and keep it. He might let her fall, or he might catch her. Ember wasn't sure which was worse.

Staying upright among hidden roots and dead branches occupied her working thoughts, a pleasant break from the turbulence of the morning. A lifelong habit of hiding her weaknesses from Nicu provided the drive to maintain the forced march with the Fae. Considering her day, she didn't even mind the company, though she wished they were taking her to lunch, rather than on a hunt for the Queen.

The way her luck was going, chances were even that Nicu and Branna would take her to the Fae, or to a safe place to hole up.

The thought jerked Ember's feet to a halt. Nicu didn't crash into her, stopping centimeters away.

"What is it, little hybrid?" His irritation suggested she'd stumbled multiple times, that she tripped on purpose. Anger blazed, only to drown in the pool of fear collected in her gut.

"Is this a trick?"

"What do you imagine is happening?" His voice fell as flat as his features.

"Are you taking me to Center?"

Nicu's shoulders widened. He leaned in and curved above, forced Ember to lift her chin a little more to face his imposed height.

"No." The word was dangerous. Final.

She was not allowed on Fae land. That did not mean she was safe.

"Are you taking me to the Fae?"

Nicu eased back to allow space between them.

"No." His gaze softened as he realized the purpose behind her questions. Relief fluttered, but her worry did not ease.

"Why not?"

Nicu stared at her long enough that Ember knew he wouldn't answer. That she had the answer if she thought about it.

He'd made a promise.

"Nicu," Branna snapped. "We will never catch her at this rate."

The warmth left Nicu's eyes when he looked at the necromancer.

"We need to go," he ordered, though his voice lost its sharp edge.

The forest had taken over much of the gravel road between the human neighborhood and the campground the Fae called home. An old gate marked where humans stopped maintaining the streets, placed after the Convergence. They rounded the pieces of metal, still on gravel that stretched a few more feet before hitting pavement.

Susan's house sat up on the hill, the door open. Broken, hanging by a straining middle hinge, and banging against the outside wall.

"Mom," Ember choked, and took off running. Branna tried to grab her as she passed.

"Do not touch her." Nicu's warning came as he reached Ember's side, then cut around her. His body blocked her from her mother's house. His pine and mist scent triggered memories of him placing himself between her and Brandt after the human had picked a fight at the End of the World.

"It could be dangerous," he warned.

"She's my mom!" Ember tried to go around Nicu, knowing better than him how serious it could be. Brandt could be in there. Or Tristan, intent on torturing the mother to get to the daughter.

Nicu shifted, anticipating the movement, still careful not to make contact. Ember charged him, taking advantage of his weakness. He dodged her, and she slipped past.

"Verge, Nicu, you cannot let her go in there," Branna shouted as Ember jumped over the crumbling steps at the front door. "The sunshine soul!"

Ember stopped just inside the shattered frame. The kitchen at the rear wall was vacant, the bistro table squeezed into the middle of the compact room bare. A rectangle of light poured over the back of the sofa bed directly to the left of the broken entry. Where sunlight blended into the drab illumination of the television, the Queen sat next to Susan's quiet form, the knife laying in her lap.

"Sh-she's sleeping, right?" Ember sputtered. Charlah looked up with a comforting smile.

"You escaped the fate-mages. Good. I'm sorry I couldn't save you. I was going to come back once I found a family. And look! The first person."

"Wh-what? Charlah, that's my mother."

Ember exaggerated her volume, hoping the Fae were listening, and figuring out a plan to get the Lees away from the Queen.

"Yours?" Charlah asked with a slight frown. Charlah eased

the loose edges of Susan's hair back toward the sleep mussed bun. "Are you certain? She's your opposite, very empty. She's hiding under her sadness and fear. There's so much room for me to share."

Charlah brightened, the lights within her eyes twinkling.

"Actually, it's perfect! Your shield is too strong and you're far too full of Veil magic to be family. With her as part of me, we can be best friends, instead!"

"What are you talking about?" Ember stepped further into the house, keeping behind the sleeper sofa where Charlah held her mother hostage.

"I'm a Queen," she replied, as if that answered all questions. "I've been everywhere inside this bubble looking for a way out, and I found you! But of course I need a family. Humans don't integrate well, but I'll only need a few before I can start gathering Witches."

Charlah sighed, caressing Susan's cheek as if she was the most precious surprise. Ember's fingers wrapped the back of the couch and she locked her elbows to support weakened knees.

"She truly is the most delicious. So wide open." Charlah leaned forward, appearing as if she might kiss Susan on the forehead. Gentle fingers cradled her quartz crystal pendant.

"No!" Ember screamed when the Queen's sharp, biting nails scraped Susan's cheek.

Nicu pulled Ember against himself, careful to keep contact limited to clothing. He flung their bodies over the couch, onto the weak mattress. Their combined weight created a wave of broken springs. Charlah was knocked back into the small bistro set in the middle of the room, the aged aluminum collapsing beneath her. With his free arm, Nicu reached for Susan and pulled her in, keeping her from crashing to the floor with the Queen.

Branna entered, bringing her shadows with her. Charlah's

growled shout echoed against the concrete walls. The tiny stars within her eyes brightened. Her skin glowed.

Branna's shadows did not fade with the growing light. They lunged for the Queen as if they had weight, black serpents intent on constricting her in darkness. One brushed Charlah and she scrambled away.

Charlah blurred, her body static while filling with kinetic energy.

"Branna!" Ember called out. The warning came too late. Charlah used her built up speed to thrust past Branna, knocking the Fae into the wall as the Queen raced from the house. Branna cursed, pushed herself through the gaping hole of the entry to follow.

Nicu eased off the screeching mattress. Ember flipped her body around so she was head to head with her mother. She traced the skin beside a thin scratch on Susan's cheek. Her mom's eyes fluttered open with the contact.

There was something different in them. They were bright.

"Ember, what are you doing?"

Ember sat up and backed to the opposite edge of the mattress, Nicu watching from the foot of the bed.

"Mom, are you okay?"

"Yes, of course I'm okay," Susan answered, her voice steady.

Susan's attention flickered around the small house. Ember looked toward Nicu, lips parted with a question he had no answer for.

"You cannot stay here," Nicu said, an echo of both his and Susan's words from five weeks ago.

"I know," Ember barked. "But I need to make sure she's okay, first."

Nicu shifted from combat ready to body guard stiff. "I mean both of you, little hybrid. We cannot leave Susan here for the sunshine soul to find her again."

"Charlah," Ember offered her name, though he must have

overheard the entire conversation through the broken door. Ember turned to Susan, willing to do anything to keep her safe. Even work with Nicu. "I'm sorry, Mom, but Nicu is right. We have to go."

Fear flickered through Susan's eyes and then they clouded for a moment. Ember tensed, bracing for that hidden switch to swap her mother back to the shell she'd been for so long.

Not this time. This time, her mom raised her chin and squared her shoulders, ready to take on the challenge.

"Whatever you want, sweetheart."

Ember's throat tightened. She leaped at her mother. The burning pleasure that came when Susan returned the hug with all the strength in her thin, tired arms was worth every moment of the last five weeks, just to have a few moments with this version of her mom.

16

DEVI

*D*evi stared into the space between her height and Aaron's bent, kneeling body.

So he'd seen the strange Wizard and survived, remembering just enough to cause problems.

How much did his father remember? What did the Wizard want to accomplish? Who was he looking for?

Aaron stirred and Devi took a half-step back. In removing the Wizard's memory spell, she'd also stripped him of the Fae glamour. The untangling lasted nearly an hour, and it had worn him out. His back expanded between the exhausted curve of his shoulders until the fabric of his puffer coat tightened, and then deflated again with each cycle of breath.

Devi returned her gems to her bracelets, examining her own resources. Her body strained from standing in one place for so long. Fatigue nipped at the edges of her energy, but adrenaline sustained her.

"Are you okay?"

Devi's subdued tone betrayed her caution. She had removed the sugar coating on Aaron's perceptions about mages, with no concept of how it affected him. Her only example was Brandt. Granted, Aaron was a far more stable human being, but Devi didn't want to take any chances.

Aaron, at least, had exposure to magic. Her mother painted a charm on his chest. Then Chase healed the stab wound Brandt gave him. Perhaps involvement with mages and the Trimarked Child would be enough.

Devi hoped so for her safety, and because she'd only caught glimpses of the freed memories. The intruding Wizard visited Aaron's house, but that was the extent of information gained.

"Aaron." His name jumped from her lips. Devi held her breath and choked down impatience, so her voice worked without its influence.

"I'm fine," Aaron gasped. He straightened with exaggerated effort. His hands rose from his folded knees to massage his forehead and temples before he looked up at her.

"What did you do to me?"

Devi only found confusion in his question. Relief released the irritation she'd been keeping in check.

"I cleared your mind of the Wizard's spell," she answered in half truth. No reason to explain the rest, just in case bringing it to his attention is what would cause him to snap. "He's the one who visited you and your father. I'm hoping you'll be able to tell me more than a few jumbled sentences at this point."

"I didn't notice any magic," Aaron argued. Devi rolled her eyes.

"Why? Because you've seen a handful of spells, you think you know how it all works?" Aaron blanched and started to stand up, then glanced at her quickly. Usually the pause to ask her permission gratified or amused Devi. Today, it was another delay.

"Get up and talk to me," she demanded.

"Kneel. Get up," Aaron muttered under his breath as he stood and brushed at the dark denim over his knees. Devi crossed her arms and allowed it for the moment, though her toe tapped against the broken road.

Devi collected each word of Aaron's experience, highlighting every detail he let slip.

"So besides the memory spell, he cast a glamour to make his eyes look human. Tall, thin, funny hat." Devi pursed her lips and her attention drifted to the north. Not toward No Man's Land, but to the hollow that rested underneath.

Saturated with the powers of Trifecta, the cave was Devi's preferred go-to space when she encountered a tough problem. Meditation within the magic facilitated her brain as she worked through puzzles, helping her pinpoint details she might have missed, otherwise. This puzzle had the quality of needing that extra boost.

But what to do with Aaron? He shouldn't wander without supervision until she understood how he acted, free of the spell that had kept him from thinking too hard.

"I have somewhere to go," she told him. "You should come with me."

"Because I can help?"

Devi fought off the urge to snap that she would never need a human's aid. She didn't want to offend him.

"To keep guard," she decided. "We shouldn't involve anyone else at this point, but I know a place where I might find answers."

"About Brandt, too?" Aaron asked. Devi's scowl was justified.

"In the sense that he's probably with the Wizard, yes," she acknowledged, then turned to dismiss the conversation and get them on their way. Aaron caught up with her remarkably quickly and with little effort. She glanced at him, but couldn't tell much from his profile.

"Look," he said, "I know everyone is worried about the Wizard, and I get it. You're a mage, he's a mage, and all that. But you have to recognize there's a human aspect of this, too."

"You mean because of your father," Devi replied.

"Yeah, in part. Dad feels guilty and wants to make it right. With the way Brandt disappeared, my dad insists on talking to him face to face. If it was any other runaway, they could show up to explain they're fine. Maybe some of them should, just to get us past this moment. But we can't find Brandt, and my dad won't give up, which means he will come looking." Aaron shrugged. "And you should care, because you're the one who lost him without telling anyone."

The accusation stung, in part because it hadn't been her decision to keep Brandt's disappearance a secret, but her mother's. It also picked at her conscience because it was true. Brandt had been given to her, and that meant she owned the responsibility. It's why she'd found Nicu this morning.

It was unhelpful to focus on the past. Their present held different challenges, and she had a plan to do something about them. Devi stopped when they reached the river bank above the entrance to the cave tunnel. Her secret that she didn't want Aaron anywhere near. But he might still turn on her, on all mages, now that the glamour was gone. He had to be close in case she needed to knock him out and get him somewhere safe.

"Listen, I want to know where Brandt is, too. I don't want him ruining everything." Aaron blanched, and Devi backed off that track, choosing different words to reassure the human she was on his side. "The Wizard who brought him in is a bigger threat, but I assure you, Brandt is a priority. I agree he needs to be found, with or without the possibility of your dad doing some digging. All that said, finding the Wizard should help us find Brandt."

She wasn't worried about that outcome, though. The Fae's spell was still on most of the human population. It appeared to work as intended. Even as humans focused on the Halfers, they were not developing a fear of magic. She simply had to keep her eye on this one. And Brandt, when she got her hands on him again.

"Yeah." Aaron took a stuttering breath. "Okay, I see your point. So what do we do?"

So far, so good. No mage-fearing Aaron in sight.

"Right now, I need you to guard my back. You can't go where I'm going. It's a straight shot, and a heads-up yell would be helpful if anything happens."

"Do you think something will?" Aaron asked, eyes wide, though at the same time his feet shifted, settling into a balanced stance. Hmm. She could work with good instincts.

"I don't know. I hope not. That's why I'm asking you to stay." Her mint-green, gemstone eyes focused on the depth of his.

"Yeah, not a problem." The words were soft, sincere. Devi offered a small smile, then slid down the dry bank and dipped behind the vines and brush that covered the front of her cave.

She paused just inside the entrance. Something was off. The air swirled around her rather than offering a cool breeze at her back. A deeper earthen smell replaced the familiar stone scent.

With quick movement, Devi grabbed the tie holding up half her curls and created a knot bun with the mass of her hair. She pushed her bracelets up her arm so they stuck in place. Witchflame danced on her palms, and she took off at a fast walk, not willing to break into a jog.

The tunnel was wide enough her fingertips could touch both sides, and high enough for someone taller than her to stand upright. Visually, the length hadn't changed. However, the atmosphere had shifted, becoming heavier with a sense of damp below her ankles.

Devi slowed to a halt when she reached the point the tunnel expanded into a spherical cave, the ground remaining level. Her chest heaved from exertion and discovery. Never clean, the cave had been clear. No water, no fungus on the walls. No plant life.

Yet, the curtain of thin, hairlike growth that greeted her

appeared long enough to belong to a mature tree. She reached above her head to caress them as she passed, gasped to see they poked through the entire ceiling. Thicker roots clung to the walls, the crumbled rocks on the floor testament to the force they used to break in.

Devi learned long ago she experienced magic differently. Along with her powers as a Witch, she saw how the molecules of magic wove together to make the world. She engaged this unique vision, desperate to know what these invaders were doing to the energy of her cave.

The air remained thick with power, and Devi's soul relaxed. The cave pulled from the natural world around it, a magnet collecting its ore. And when Devi looked at the roots, she stopped breathing.

The tree took from the magic, sucking it in, having found a never-ending food supply. But for what? There were no trees in No Man's Land.

"How did you find this place?"

Devi dropped her attention from the ceiling to the back of the cave, fingers wide, lips parted to chant. A girl stood between two thick roots that hugged the convex wall. Her pale hair drifted to her waist over the slippery fabric of her belted dress. She gripped something in her right fist, angled so it was impossible to see.

"Where did you come from?" Devi had not let down her guard during her contemplation. Aaron didn't sound the alarm. Yet this being slipped past them both and snuck up on her.

"I was exploring the Circle when I heard you talking to your human. The other humans ignore magic, but not him, which makes him very special. Then you came here, which was interesting. My brother said it was a secret."

The woman's voice rose and fell like a song hid within the spoken words. Her fingers curled so the sharp edges of her nails pressed into the granite. As she turned, Devi saw what she held.

"How do you have my knife? Who are you?"

"I'm Charlah. This isn't yours. I took it from someone else. He would have mentioned if it wasn't his."

She faced the cave, and Devi saw her eyes.

Bedtime stories meant to frighten children into good behavior rose within Devi's memory. The story of the Queen told of enslavement and the drone-like connection transmitted into her victims.

Charlah had been imprisoned in Heldu. The Queen should not be in Terra.

Devi traced a protective glyph in the air before her and felt magic settle over her skin like a fine mist. She counted up and over her arm until she found the bracelet with a repeating six stone pattern. Smoky amethyst, obsidian, shungite, quartz, hematite, yellow labradorite. She slipped it over the bracelets before it, settled it around the base of her four fingers, held it in place with her thumb, and lifted her hand between herself and the Queen.

"Ooh, you are special, aren't you? Your eyes can turn into mine when you Work." Charlah's lips drifted from a gentle smile to a pout. "Well, you won't fit into my family, will you? Too big inside."

Devi stepped back, in full agreement with the Queen's assessment, even if she wasn't certain of the reasoning.

"The boy outside, though," Charlah continued, her attention toward the tunnel as she slipped the knife between her dress and belt. "Humans don't usually make good family members, but this Veil town has surprised me. I found an empty woman, first. Now this human. He knows the most delightful things."

She lowered her voice as if sharing a delicious secret with Devi. "There's an entire group of people here with the blood of mages, but they can't sense magic at all. Can you imagine? They'll be perfect for my family, and that boy knows where to find them."

The Queen would take control of her victims' minds, forcing them to serve her and be her strength. A queen bee with her collection of drones, meant to serve only her. Icy sweat prickled, and Devi pursed her lips to hide their tremble.

"They're half breeds, not nearly the same as a full mage," she challenged. If Devi convinced the Queen to go straight to the High Priestess without any drones, there was a greater chance the coven could fight her off.

"But more fun," the Queen chimed. A gust of wind marked Charlah's disappearance. A trail cut through the length of the tunnel, similar to the magical path Devi investigated five weeks prior.

Brandt. The starfall knife. The Wizard. And now, a mutated Witch. All linked by magic-made passageways. The puzzle pieces matched, but didn't line up. She did not have the time to order them into a coherent picture.

Devi sprinted toward the river, the trail's power fading. She pushed herself after it, magical bubbles popping before her eyes as the Queen's spell disappeared before she connected.

Making paths was a branch of magic she'd never studied since Trifecta was so small. There was no time for trial-and-error Work. So she ran and focused on making a decision.

Go home, get Leona. Or save as many of the Halfers as possible and try to rescue Aaron.

If the Halfers were taken, Charlah would have an army. That Halfers could not tap into their magic side did not matter. Their Queen was more than capable. She'd be the one in control via the hive mind connection.

Devi wished she could run faster, or that she had a Fae to attach to as she'd done with Edan not long ago. When she reached the tunnel's entrance, she turned toward the east.

Aaron was not there.

She'd left him vulnerable, and was responsible for correcting her mistake.

There was no right answer here. Gather her coven of

Witches and Wizards to combat the Halfers Charlah collected. Or try to prevent Charlah from gathering her army, giving the Witches an advantage in numbers.

The Queen said Devi couldn't be family and mentioned their powers were too similar. The Halfers and the coven were vulnerable.

The Witches had her mom.

The scales tipped, and Devi sped due east, set to skirt the edge of the Circle.

Defending the Halfers might provide the best chance with the fewest casualties. The coven was more prepared to take on a threat, unexpected or not.

Devi's legs protested the speed, her lungs cramped with the distance. She hated to run. She could not stop.

17

NICU

Nicu guarded the door, and Ember guarded her mother. Susan gathered her own things while the hybrid girl's hand fluttered at her sides, ready to step in with a second's notice if needed.

Nicu had never seen the hybrid girl like this. Uncertain. A helpless glaze over her eyes. In their interactions she was full of fire, her spine steel straight. Discomfort prickled his skin and he looked away from this unexpected variation of the Trimarked Child.

The interior of the hut was cold, and not just because the door had broken. Nothing blocked the porous surface of the concrete walls. No obvious source of heat. It would do Susan good to be somewhere else for the time being. It was beneficial that Ember had moved into the Halfer's zone.

Nicu's teeth threatened to clench. It did not settle well that the better place was also the source of their injuries. Her choices should not be limited to freezing or living with bullies. Nicu would have to remind the Halfers that the Trimarked Child was under his protection.

"If you need to go after Charlah so badly, why don't you

just go?" Ember's blunt words broke into Nicu's thoughts. "I can walk my mom underground."

The hybrid girl's question had come from misinterpreting his intense study. He would not correct her, especially as he preferred the return of her combative energy.

"You have experienced that woman's speed twice. Chase will have closed the tunnels for the winter. The Halfer zone is not close enough," he challenged.

Her lips pursed into a scowl, narrowed eyes betraying her suspicion. She could use more control, yet Nicu found it expedient to be able to read her so clearly. She might doubt him, but she was willing to follow if it meant keeping her mother safe.

"I'm ready." Susan spoke as if admitting a fault rather than an intention to leave. Ember held her hand out for her mom's bag. Susan hesitated, looked around once more, and then gave Ember her luggage.

"It's just for right now," Ember soothed.

"I've always wanted to find the underground," Susan murmured, the words adding strength to her spine. Ember's color faded. Her lips parted on an unasked question. Susan smiled, unaware of her daughter's response. "There were rumors when you were born, of someone who took in the babies."

"F-for me?" Ember gasped. Susan stopped just before the door and gripped Ember with her boney hands.

"Of course not. Not that way," Susan insisted. "For family."

Susan's gray eyes shifted, almost blurred. Nicu's instincts flickered, his attention less on the outside than within.

"Family is so important," Susan continued. Nothing in her words seemed out of place. Susan's response pacified Ember. Yet, something was not right. The last time Nicu had seen Susan, she'd screamed at him to stay away, suggesting Ember was better off dead than surrounded by magic. Though her mental state had been strained at the time, her easy acquiescence now concerned him.

Nicu descended the steps, creating room for the women to exit the house. He made eye contact with Branna, who stood beside the stairs at ground level. Irritation flashed when she saw him, a sign she still held a grudge. Possibly many.

When Susan appeared, the necromancer stepped back. The rich color of her irises grew and her pupils constricted, as if she stared at something too bright.

Like sunshine.

Branna's lips parted and Nicu crowded her side, his own lips thinned in wordless communication meant to encourage her silence.

The odd Witch had done something that made Susan's spirit brighter, judging by Branna's reaction. Magic, as Nicu knew it, had not been involved. He lacked a spell to grab on to, or traces of energy to seize. They needed to retreat, to get Ember someplace safe where they could study Susan in hopes of discovering her affliction. He blinked slowly, acknowledging what Branna had seen, a sign to the other Fae. Stay alert without tipping off the hybrid girl, who had not noticed the changes in her mother.

Nicu led the way around the corner of the old maintenance building, setting his pace to keep himself within reach of Ember, who guided Susan. Branna trailed behind, her eyes brushed with shadow.

Nicu ignored the heavy steel door at the side of the concrete structure, and took a path up the hill and behind the tree line. They did not want to be seen along the road together, particularly with curiosity growing within the humans. Ember followed without challenge, the worried gazes she sent toward her mother proof she obeyed on Susan's behalf, not Nicu's.

"We're going to where the Halfers live," Susan reaffirmed. Nicu stopped his tongue from demanding Ember didn't engage. They needed to act as if there was a spy in their midst.

Yet he could not risk a delay, which an argument with the hybrid girl would certainly cause.

"Do you think we'll see the babies?" Susan asked. At least her natural tone was quiet and Nicu did not have to concern himself over whether a nearby human might overhear.

"Um, no, Mom. They don't keep small kids where we're going."

"Have you seen them?"

The question dripped with years of suffering and hope. Susan blinked wet eyes, a hand pressed to her heart, the other gripping Ember's. The hybrid girl studied the ground, her hair falling forward with each step.

"No," Ember answered.

The anguish in her answer was more contained than Susan's. It affected Nicu more than the old woman's. He turned away, smoothed his features.

"Oh. I want to meet her," Susan sighed.

"Who?" Ember asked.

"The one who cared for the babies. Halfers didn't exist twenty years ago to do it. I always wondered if I knew her."

"You wouldn't," Branna answered from her position at the rear, no apology for Nicu in the forceful tone as she shared information. "It wasn't a human."

"It couldn't have been anyone else," Susan argued. "Magic has no love for humans."

"Humans have no love for magic,' Branna shot back. Nicu turned to catch the flutter of tattoos over skin.

Too late, Nicu recognized her choice to speak was not focused on the now, but on the death of her mother, and Branna's own rebirth. The event caused, in part, by the human woman she followed. High Magic meant for the Trimarked Child she guarded.

"Branna," he warned, a twist of apology in the growled purr. He could not release her, not when the hybrid girl stood arm and arm with danger.

They passed the last of the maintained properties and took to the pockmarked street. Bits of wheat-gold weeds had curled and dried after their summer's siege on this forgotten stretch. Boarded-up houses appeared empty, even to Nicu's trained eye. He wasn't certain how many housed the unwanted offspring begotten by parents of different races.

Most of these children were half human, half Witch, as the coven interacted consistently within human lives, and lived by a flexible code of conduct. Human and Fae youths had been noted by those who studied this group from afar, noting peculiarities in features, and via discreet scans of their life force. None were of Fae motherhood, and no male Fae claimed the crime. Knowing their numbers was not vital to Nicu's duty, so there had been no reason to cultivate or investigate it.

As they picked their way across the road, a door opened to their left. Their small group stopped as if with previous agreement, and turned toward the sound while making none of their own.

Aaron stepped out of the house. His bouncing stride popped him from the porch to the dead, overgrown yard. He scanned their faces, held onto Susan. His usual cocky smile was missing, and did not offer a greeting.

Branna hummed a single, declaring note of confirmation.

He was afflicted.

Doors along the street opened, one after another. Halfers seeped from their depths.

"Mom." The surprise in Ember's voice alerted Nicu to her movement. Susan had gathered her strength and pulled Ember toward Aaron. Nicu's fingertips warmed with a desire to grab the Trimarked girl, but hesitated as he remembered their last touch had resulted in the ability to read each other's thoughts.

"Branna, secure the Child," he ordered.

The necromancer's shade rose from the ground, wrapped around Ember and locked them together. It skimmed Susan, who startled at the contact and let go of her daughter, shaking her hand as if burned. Branna's shadows continued to do what Nicu could not, and they pulled Ember to safety between the two Fae, ignoring Ember's shout.

Nicu observed the fuzzy eyed crowd. How many shadows could Branna control at once? He'd noted throughout the day her power had grown and skills multiplied. He did not consider these changes through Wist's lens of suspicion, but as a valuable tool for protecting the Trimarked Child.

Within the dilated pupils of those who opposed them, a haze sharpened into a glow, as if pieces of the sunshine soul infected their bodies. As if the Queen used all their eyes.

Branna's shadows would not be enough. Nicu's strength would not be enough. He needed another way to keep the hybrid girl safe.

The talisman sat heavily at the base of his skull, waiting for his decision.

18

EMBER

*E*mber slapped and scratched at the corporeal shadows wrapped around her body, strained to get to her mother.

"Let me go!" She didn't know why her mom had pulled her toward Aaron and the Halfers. Perhaps Susan had been excited to meet the mixed blood kids she'd imagined for so long. Ember wasn't as eager to join the group who tried to trigger her traumas.

In fact, why were Aaron and the Halfers lined up as if to greet them?

Ember's attention, so focused on Susan, zoomed out to take in the scene. Halfers, stiff as statues, outside in a large gathering, all seen together. A human boy at their center, the only one to cross into the road, to match his position up with theirs. Actions that were completely against the Halfers' usual movements. As far as Ember knew, being so visible was a cardinal sin among them. Secrecy and protection were at their core, and they certainly wouldn't have elected Aaron as their spokesperson.

Susan at Aaron's side made the least sense of all.

Ember ceased struggling against Branna and studied her

mother, seeing the clarity in Susan's eyes. Her pupils glowed in the afternoon sunshine. Her features were less drawn. Even Susan's frown was soft as she examined the shadows that held Ember, her posture uncurled.

Oh, crap, she hadn't been paying attention. Nicu had been prepared, ordering Branna to secure Ember. Why had he let her get away with her misconception?

"Isn't it lovely?" Charlah's melodious voice preceded her as she approached Ember from the crowd of Halfers. Nicu shifted, blocking the Queen from Ember like a knight on a chessboard. Ember shot a glare toward Branna, tried to convey she knew better now. The Fae did not release her.

Charlah clicked her tongue. "I was talking to my best friend," she pouted. "Please move, or I might poke you with my knife again."

"My knife."

Devi's breathless announcement came from the direction of the Circle. She approached from behind Aaron with a heavy rise and fall of her chest, limp curls free of her bun. She studied Aaron for a moment, took in his stiff posture, then focused on Charlah.

"I told you," Charlah chimed. "I did not take this from you."

"No," Devi agreed, having rounded Aaron and Susan to join Ember and the two Fae. "He took it from me a long time ago."

If there had been any doubt Tristan might have been her father, Devi's confirmation that he'd been in Trifecta and able to steal the starfall knife, confirmed it. The Witch would have been very young, but Ember believed the woman who noticed the smallest of details.

Ember tugged at the shadows, irritated that she stared at Nicu's back and couldn't watch the play of emotions across Charlah's face. Worse, all she saw of her mother was the edge of her arm, with Branna and Devi in the way.

"Branna, let me go," Ember hissed.

Charlah appeared behind Branna, her movements missed by all, and caused a ripple of shifting positions in response. Nicu's heat radiated into Ember as he stepped close, but not around. She swallowed down the regret that he no longer stood between her and the Queen.

"Yes, let her go, dead one. Your powers aren't so strong after all. Just a little sting. Nothing to be afraid of."

"Really?" Branna asked, and freed Ember. Shadows pooled at the Halfers' feet, collected from the foundations of the houses, the roots of the trees, and from their own bodies. The glow within their pupils increased. The Halfers shifted, their faces twisted and sweat dripped, but they did not try to escape the moving darkness. Inky tendrils rushed toward Charlah, who curled her lip but stood her ground. Stars swirled in the deep galaxies of her eyes, and the shadows burst apart.

Branna cried out, dropped to one knee, her spine arched. Scythe-shaped tattoos retracted and stuttered into their resting positions.

"See?" Charlah asked, standing over the necromancer. "Powers in a cage. Why do they do that here, lock up all your capabilities? They're foolish. Magic doesn't die. Everything breaks out. It just takes time." Charlah's full lips curled. "Lucky for me, I'm out of my prison and you aren't, and now I can get my friend."

Vertigo hit Ember. The insides of her brain contorted, her stomach clenched on bile. By the time her vision cleared, pinching pain radiated from her arm. She faced Nicu's fiery glower instead of his wide, protective back. Charlah had dragged her away from her guardians to stand with Aaron and Susan. Three against three, with the Trimarked Child as the prize.

A deep growl vibrated within Nicu as Aaron approached. The human's hand gripped Nicu's bicep. Nicu's free arm swung up and around Aaron's temple. An involuntary gasp escaped Ember, anticipating the golden boy's fall.

Instead, Aaron ducked the punch and hit the darkened shoulder on Nicu's jacket, then backhanded him against his ear. The Fae grunted. He took a step away from Aaron, forfeiting the fight.

"This is you," Nicu accused the Queen.

Aaron backed away as bell tone laughter danced from Charlah's lips.

"You have all of them?" Devi snapped, scanning the Halfer-littered street as if noticing them for the first time.

"Isn't it amazing? My family shares their strength with each other! And your mom is part of it," Charlah beamed toward Ember, whose jaw dropped. She looked between the Queen, Aaron and her mother, realization chilling her bones.

"A Queen," Ember whispered. Like a bee, and the Halfers were her servant drones.

"You understand now!" Charlah exclaimed, as if this were the most exciting thing that had happened all day. "So I'll keep your mom. You'll love it. She's more awake than she's been in a decade. I can protect her from getting buried in the past. She'll be your old mom again, and we'll all be happy."

Ember's heart swelled painfully with its next beat. Her body filled with pinpricks of electricity that snapped blue at her fingertips.

"Ow!" Charlah hissed. A cry escaped Ember when Charlah twisted her arm at the shoulder in an effort to step away without letting go. "I don't need to absorb your power, remember? We'll use it later."

"Ember, calm down," Susan counseled. Her voice soothing, her eyes steady despite the magic happening all around her.

Ember gawked. Whatever Charlah claimed happened within the hive mind, it wasn't the entire truth. Her mother would never be okay with a show of power, especially from Ember.

Charlah squealed, blasting Ember's hearing. Branna loomed, encompassed in darkness. Tattoos fanned out as scythe-shaped feathers coated nearly all visible skin, the points climbing up her neck to mask her face.

"You are not this strong!" Charlah shrieked at the necromancer. She released Ember, and walked backward on stilted legs.

Nicu had eased around the diversion, successfully avoiding Aaron and Susan, who were preoccupied with Branna's shadows. He gently caught Ember's coat, pulling her away from Charlah.

"We need to go." His voice vibrated just within her range of hearing in the one ear Charlah had not damaged.

"My mom," she breathed, reaching for Susan.

"She is not your mom."

"Her body is," Ember hissed in return.

Nicu frowned and took in the scene. Ember slipped behind him, then around to her mother. Susan hadn't moved without direction from her Queen.

Aaron wasn't there for her to grab. He stood beside his Queen, who had retreated to the curb to avoid Branna's halo of night. Midnight melted from the necromancer's body and formed a hollow ring around those in the street, trapping Susan with Ember, Devi and the Fae. The concentrated darkness thickened the outward width of the ring, reaching not just for Charlah, but toward the Halfers.

Charlah vanished. The shadows' expansion paused with the Queen's disappearance, though her drones remained.

"They are her hive," Devi grunted, a fine mist of sweat coating her skin. She stood behind Branna, hands held out toward the necromancer. "Hold it."

Branna nodded, her trembling fists at her sides.

Ember gasped at their show of collaboration. She couldn't see the magic, but remembering how Charlah swatted away Branna's shadows earlier, Devi must be enhancing the dark energy somehow. Ice settled into her gut and she looked toward her mother.

Charlah controlled Susan's mind. Aaron's and the Halfers, as well. A Queen so powerful, a Fae and Witch deemed it necessary to work together against her.

Ember turned to Aaron, her chest aching with the need to reach out to him, but there was nothing in his face that suggested he had control of his body, or that he'd be able to listen.

Without warning, the Halfers ran northeast into the forest. Susan whimpered. Her feet moved toward the shadows, then away. She tried to follow. She was too afraid of the darkness.

Aaron was the last of the drones to leave, jogging at the rear. Not looking back.

Tears pricked Ember's eyes, and she squeezed her lids together. There had to be a way to help him and her mom.

"Can Branna's magic break Charlah's hold?" she asked.

"No," Devi spoke with speed brought on by effort.

"But they can bind her," Nicu said, an offer and an order.

"I can let go, now?" Branna wheezed.

"Yes," Devi agreed.

With a shared shudder, the women released their spells. Branna's brow wrinkled in displeasure as a small shadow crept along Susan's body in response to Nicu's command. Ember's mom screamed with contact. The sound cut off once the dark band wrapped around her head.

"It's hurting her," Ember choked.

"Not much, according to Charlah," Devi reminded her. "Just a sting. This is the only way you get to keep her. Deaf and blind."

The mages showed no signs of give, all in agreement. Ember swallowed and nodded. Nicu carried Susan, awkward but steady with the dead weight of a body not helping support itself.

"Where do we go?" Branna asked, her tone deepened to protect from echoes. "We have to move before Charlah figures out the strength of those shadows came from Devi's illusion."

"And before I have to cast another spell on the fly without my crystals." Devi blotted her face with the cuff of her sweater.

Ember trembled, her arms wrapped around her torso, fingers tapping furiously against the silky fabric of her puff jacket. Where would they go?

"This way." Chase's voice rang over the street, the answer to her silent question. A door opened, decoy boards sticking out from the edges. He waved them in, wary eyes on Susan.

Chase allowed everyone to pass through, but stopped Nicu who had brought up the rear. Ember spun on her heel just beyond his gate-keeping form.

"Chase—" Ember tried, but the Halfer cut her off with a backward reach of his hand.

"You're certain she's safe?"

"Do you think the hybrid girl will leave her?" Nicu countered.

Chase's lips thinned. His nod jerked in sharp, unwelcome acknowledgement.

"Let's go." He admitted the Fae and his burden, then closed the door against the early afternoon light.

19

AARON

The Queen called to Aaron's soul. She urged him away from the broken road and the run-down houses into the cool, deep shadows of the late autumn forest. The trees stood tall in red and dressed in green, their thick branches ready for the snow that would arrive in the coming weeks.

He ran with the Halfers at Charlah's command. They passed the Witch border without detection, proof their Queen protected them from eyes that would have never allowed the trespass of so many to go unchallenged. As they continued, the stress of needing to run lessened, the speed of their feet slowed. They shifted toward the north, then back to the west until they walked quietly into the dead clearing. Aaron had known the name of this place, but didn't remember now, especially when a large pine tree at its center brought confusion rather than memory.

Many of the Halfers stayed outside the triangular clearing, finding fallen trees to rest against, ground to collapse on. Their star-blind vision fixed on the ethereal figure dressed in pale green. Aaron was not invited to sit. Instead, he stood where instructed, within easy reach of his Queen.

Charlah paced between giant trunks, swinging a knife that sparked a bright spot in the opaque mist within Aaron's mind. A phantom pain flashed in his thigh and he remembered the blade had been the cause. He stared at the weapon. Pictures of the attack challenged the cloud. He remembered the hand around the grip. The face of his attacker stuck in the haze.

Charlah stopped pacing and focused on him. The fog thickened.

"Not yet, silly boy. Not yet."

Memories swirled in with the words, though if they were from his perspective or hers, he wasn't certain. He sat on the high bank of a river. The Queen came before him. The universes in her eyes captivated him, and he found himself lost in the stars.

A separate moment. Inside a house. Excitement rose. There were people they could make family. Well, not that human one. Charlah collected another family member. One of the humans appeared too close. The Queen didn't want more humans. She turned and wrapped her hands around the girl's neck —

Charlah hummed, the pressure behind his eyes increased, and memories were pushed away from his conscious thoughts.

"Shh," she soothed. "It's okay."

She took that memory away, deciding it wasn't important for him to have. All she let Aaron remember was she had important information for him. Maybe something to do with that knife, or one of the people he couldn't remember. It didn't matter, yet. She needed help before she'd share.

"Is the family big enough?" Odd, how the question came, though he hadn't found the memory. Charlah sifted through in his mind. She angled her head, and a smile blossomed on her lips.

"I knew you were exceptional," she purred. "Millions out in the world, and you were right here in this bubble waiting for me. How did you get free of that Fae spell on human minds?"

A cranberry haired Witch breached before diving back into

forgotten memories. Charlah straightened with excitement, clapped her hands around her grip on the knife.

"How lovely! The earth-mage helped me without even knowing it. She's who I was supposed to be. Except, someone is stopping her from believing."

Whatever she meant behind her words, Charlah didn't see fit to share the secret with her family. The mystery failed to stir any other memories or questions for Aaron, so he let it go into the fog, waiting to learn what his Queen wanted next.

"Hmm. Do the earth-mages know what they have in her? I wonder if they realize what they trapped? I'll have the answers soon enough!" she chirped. "Tell me about where they live?"

Every mind within the clearing lit up through Aaron's own. Information drifted to his Queen and to him. He connected with the hive mind to answer in his own way. Instantly, the Halfers' thoughts faded. Charlah fixated on Aaron.

"You've been to so many places in the Circle!" she exclaimed, approaching his space with a flush of joy on her cheeks. "So special. I would make you my consort, if it wasn't for our arrangement. What do you think?" she asked, easing in until her breasts brushed his chest. Black eyes blended with long lashes, and galaxies spun.

Aaron's mind remained blank, his lips silent. He endured the power of the Queen as she filtered his thoughts. Images of him by her side. A family of unimaginable strength. The hive increased her potency, giving all for the good of their Queen. With Charlah to care for them, they no longer had to struggle to live, as she would be their home. They wouldn't have to negotiate their place amongst the different races when everyone was loyal to the Queen. Aaron stood before her. Not a drone, but a leader. A partner. An extension of her power when he had no hope of gaining magical ability any other way.

"Beautiful, isn't it?" she whispered aloud as her thoughts infected him. "It's what you've wanted. Peace. Belonging. A place for everyone."

Another image flashed, one of Aaron's own. A dark-haired girl with silvery eyes.

"Oh," Charlah pouted. "No, not her. But she can be a friend, if she behaves. She can't keep nipping me with that energy she carries."

"Where is she?"

"Caught behind that necromancer's shadows," Charlah spat. "Our family is magnificent, but we cannot fight off death with people who cannot cast spells."

"The necromancer will bring death?"

Charlah studied Aaron for a moment, her power probing his mind, trying to judge his intentions. If he had any, he wasn't aware of them, buried as they were under the fog.

"You see this tree?" she asked, directing him toward the pine at the center of the dead space that stretched half the height of the surrounding redwoods. "It's a very hungry tree, and my brother thinks my oversized soul would be perfect for it. My brother told me he already fed it one spirit. But I don't want to go into the silly old tree. Spreading my spirit out will help keep my brother from feeding me to it, but he won't stop trying. What we need is a trade. To capture souls rich enough, we have to be stronger."

"So we'll grow the family." Aaron's mind formed images of himself and the Halfers, growing their numbers with faceless others. Charlah caught the thought and refined it for him, topping each of the new additions with a different shade of red hair.

"Exactly. And you have proven the most helpful. With your map of the Circle, we'll be able to grow the family in no time!" Charlah shifted so her body faced south. "That way. We need to go before the earth-mage girl who wants my knife warns them."

The Halfers rose from their resting places. Warmth caressed Aaron's mind, bringing with it an image of himself by

Charlah's side. He approached her, but stopped short of coming abreast, standing behind her despite the invitation.

"You are quite strong," Charlah murmured. "I wonder if you would like to go into the tree?"

An alarm flashed. His body struggled, wanting to move away but stuck in place by the power of Charlah's soul.

"Well, you would finally find Brandt, since he's already in there."

Aaron gripped the name she'd given him before it drifted back into the fog, squeezed it into the small moment of consciousness he still claimed apart from Charlah's overwhelming presence. As Charlah directed them out of the clearing, he was sorry to leave behind the starving tree.

20

EMBER

*E*mber twisted her hands in front of her and split her attention between Nicu and Chase. This morning the exception, she had never seen these two men together. She hadn't been in the mood earlier to study their interactions. Thinking back to her power leak, she winced. They probably hadn't been attentive to each other, anyway.

Chase directed them through the small house he'd hid in, one used for long-term food storage. Devi spoke a few sharp words that he cut off with a growled demand to be quiet. It was the deep lines around his lips and the banked fury in his eyes that kept them silent, even as he opened a broom closet with a crawl space door in the floor. He gestured everyone to follow, then dropped through it.

Devi tucked her arms and took a step, floating more than falling. Branna went next, landing seconds after the Witch. Ember tapped fingertips against her thighs, uncertain how they'd get Susan to descend. After some cajoling, her blinded mother eased herself down, Chase only helping after Ember pushed the request through gritted teeth.

Ember scrambled after. Nicu, as always, was the last in

line. She slipped her arm into her mother's. The necromancer sneered at the contact. If it had been up to her, Susan would have followed the Queen.

Ember pressed into Susan's side, the packed-earth escape tunnel meant for single file travel. The energy reverberating between Chase at the front and Nicu at the back sent tremors through her. Not magical in nature, their force of self was nearly as tangible. It was miraculous that they weren't creating sparks of their own.

The passageway wasn't much longer than the one under Ember's old house. The tunnel dead ended into a flat, wooden panel. Chase shoved a skeleton key into the sunken lock, and turned it with a short, forceful twist. He stood, white knuckled, head bowed, then faced those who followed him.

"I will kill you if anyone learns about this." He glared into every pair of eyes under the ceiling mounted lights. His attention hardened on Susan. When he looked at Ember, the muscles in his jaw bulged and his lids lowered on a sigh. Chase used the key to push open the wooden panel. The piece popped open, letting light in along with echoing screams.

Devi hissed on her inhale and pressed forward. A squeal cut through the air and Ember's mouth fell agape. She'd thought Chase's threat of death had been metaphorical. As she gawked at the children of varying ages playing tag, she knew he meant every word.

The passage exited left of the wall-mounted kitchenette and island bar. The club side of the door was plastered in thin concrete and closed in line with the gentle convex curve of the cylindrical room. The edges mimicked inconsistencies in the surrounding wall, including an irregularly shaped hole at waist level, the perfect size for the skeleton key Chase used to lock the panel into place.

The system of tunnels was built to collect hundreds of gallons of floodwater as snow melted from the mountains. With less precipitation because of climate change, the channels had been dry for decades. The Halfers claimed them for ease of travel under the city, and they used this large holding chamber as a hangout space during the warmer months. Apparently, it turned into a nursery for the winter.

A squeaky wail cut across the laughter. Ember's eyes roamed toward the boxing ring that had been fenced, and five cribs placed inside. A female teen entertained a toddler duo, laughing at their antics as she caressed a rounded belly. A second caretaker was younger than Ember, familiar as he lifted the crying infant from its bed. When he turned, he proved to be the boy who'd gone on his first raid with her all those weeks ago and couldn't stop babbling about car tailpipes.

"This way," Chase ordered as they crossed back to his favorite horseshoe shaped booth. They passed the lounge area where older Halfers gathered in small groups. Another snored on a couch, an arm flung over his eyes. One of the ten visible doors that lined the outer chamber walls opened, and three Halfers tumbled in, exhausted and sweat stained.

"Some are still finding their way back," Chase explained. "That crazy gnome only wanted mixed-bloods, and let the humans run. Except for —"

Chase stopped his words when the game of tag came too close, or because he simply didn't want to continue. Another older caretaker nearer to Ember's age approached, her eyes accusing, her lips trembling.

"What are they doing here?"

Chase held up a hand to stop her. "Zoe, please. Our problems are bigger than these people," he informed her. "Are the doors unlocked?"

"Most of them, I'd guess, based on traffic. Keegan isn't back yet."

"There must be more out there, then."

"They'll be fine," Zoe soothed.

"Yeah," Chase's answer was tight, confident. "Keegan's a survivor. He'll make sure the others find their way home."

The growl in his voice reminded Ember of the tone he'd used with Aaron over coffee when he ranted about eyes turning blind. She wondered if that had anything to do with Keegan, the goofy boxer who had given up his room to her because he tried to stop a fight, but got her punched instead.

Chase wouldn't answer her if she asked. Keegan didn't deserve her prying. Ember shifted her grip on her mother, the woman who hadn't abandoned her. Susan lost herself, but never raised a hand to her daughter.

Being Trimarked wasn't the worst thing in the world.

"We need food," Chase murmured on a sigh, eyes flickering to Ember when her stomach growled. Ember ignored both the noise and his detection of it.

Zoe nodded and herded the children into the kitchen with the promise of snacks. Chase didn't choose his usual spot at the center of the curve. He took one of the outer two chairs instead. Nicu grabbed the second chair. He helped Susan slide in before Ember followed. Before either Devi or Branna shifted the line deeper, Nicu dropped into his seat, cutting off access, holding Ember between himself and Susan.

With a raised brow, Chase made room so Branna and Devi could enter on his side of the curved bench. Branna went first to be near Susan. Devi sat at the furthest edge, not interested in scooting anywhere. Ember stared at Nicu, noticed the flexed muscle in his jaw, and decided to follow Chase's lead, and let it go.

"Now that everyone is comfortable, what the verge is going on up there?" Chase demanded, his hushed words setting the tone of the meeting. "I popped up after getting the Clubhouse ready for the kids. The mixed-blooded were brainwashed. The runaways scrambled. Sadie—" He choked, rubbed his closed eyes, then cleared his throat and faced Ember.

"Sadie was a bitch, but didn't deserve to be strangled to death."

Ember's trembling fingers covered her mouth. The sound

of a door opening burst through the room. Chase turned to find Keegan escorting a few more stragglers, a deep breath allowing his shoulders to fall a few inches.

"Branna," Nicu commanded.

"They're all clean."

"What does that fading mean?" Chase barked.

"It has to do with the Queen," Devi answered.

"Gnome royalty?" Chase rocked back in his chair, eyes narrowed at the Witch he did not fully trust.

"Not at all." Devi ignored the insult and rested her forearms on the table, angled so she could fiddle with the stones on her bracelets. "She's a mistake. An experiment gone wrong."

Ember flinched with Devi's confirmation. Nicu's eyes flickered to her, having caught the quiver. Ember leaned into the patched vinyl upholstery and shook her hair forward.

Zoe rushed in with a platter of meat and cheese sandwiches and a pitcher of water. Two of the older kids carried scratched plastic cups. Once everything was served, she swept the kids away with shushing noises even though they hadn't made a peep.

"What does that mean?" Chase snapped at Devi. He grabbed a sandwich and leaned carelessly across Nicu to shove it at Ember. From her slouch, she reached up to rescue the food before he dropped it in her lap. "None of this helps the Halfers."

Branna had the second sandwich, a bite in her mouth as she poured herself water. Nicu ignored the meal. Susan refused it. Chase focused on Devi rather than eating.

"Some Witches and Wizards thought they figured out the formula to make a goddess," Devi continued. "Instead, they made a Queen. She can split herself up and gain a hold of people's minds. Lots of people. She creates a hive mind."

"So we're all in danger?" Chase's question vibrated from his chest, and his wide eyes focused on the kids across the room.

"Not all of us," Branna countered. "She fears me. I think Ember's immune."

"She says I'm too full," Ember muttered.

"Me, too," Devi surprised the table. "She said she prefers to leave humans out of it, though I guess she needed at least Susan and Aaron before she was strong enough to go after the mixed-bloods."

"You met her before this showdown?" Chase asked, and noticed Ember hadn't gotten water. He poured her a cup, then glared until she swallowed her bite and took a drink. Whenever she visited the Clubhouse, Chase usually bugged her about getting food or water, but when had he become such a nursemaid? Lucky for him, she desperately needed both today, and had no desire to deny herself.

"Yes. When she collected Aaron." Devi spoke through tight lips, loath to admit mistakes. "He was with me while I checked something out. She collected him before introducing herself."

"That fading human boy's luck." Chase covered his eyes with the heels of his hands. His fingers gripped the long strands of his hair, then dropped to the wooden tabletop. "What else? What do we do?"

"I don't know." Devi stared at her bracelets through the reluctant confession.

Ember leveraged herself into better posture.

"Charlah wants a big family, so she's strong enough to get out of Trifecta." Every eye at the table turned to her. Her lip twitched, and she pursed her mouth before the snarl escaped. Why was it such a surprise she had something to offer?

"Ah, the Queen's best friend," Branna drawled. Ember huffed and refused to look at the Fae.

"It means we have time to figure out how to help them. I don't think she'll hurt anyone who is her family."

"Aaron," Chase murmured. Ember nodded, and glanced at her mother.

"But they also increase her power, so not much more time," Devi mused.

Susan gasped. She bumped Ember and tried to stand up, the table keeping her bent as she attempted to scramble out of the booth. Ember slid across the slick seat. She reached out and grasped Susan's hand with an instinctive drive to grab something for balance. Susan shoved, and Ember threw out her other arm. Her shoulder slammed into Nicu's torso as he moved to steady her and block Susan.

Ember's palm slapped Nicu's. She gripped on instinct, skin to skin, fingertips pressed to the Living Ink on the back of his hand.

Blue light flared within Ember's mind. Sparks ignited at contact, then through her to Susan.

Don't touch me, her thoughts hissed between herself and Nicu.

Release me, Nicu growled in return.

Ember couldn't let go. In fact, she gripped him tighter as their connection forged a link between them and Susan. Ember fell into her mother's clouded mind, lost with no sense of direction. One thought brightened against the dark fog.

Follow my Queen. The Witches will be family. Follow my Queen.

Nicu grunted and stood from his chair, knocking it back. With his gain in height, he lifted Ember out of the bench seat and away from her mom's reach. Susan fell without Ember's support. Chase sprung across the table to keep her from bashing her head on the wood.

Nicu dropped Ember's hand as if he'd touched fire. Ember moaned, her hands digging into her temples to hold the splitting pieces together. Her ears rang high and her vision blackened.

A chill point of pressure began above her brow and spread in a cool, healing blanket over the pain. Ember blinked open to find herself supported by Nicu's arm around her waist. Chase held two fingers on her forehead. The rest clutched a polished, hazy green gemstone that channeled his healing magic.

Nicu checked her pupils, saw they were clean. He let her use his strength until she'd regained hers before releasing her.

"Charlah called her hive to the Circle," Ember shared.

Ember blinked to clear the leftover blur from her eyes and tracked down Susan who was tied into a sitting position with more of Branna's shadows. The table rocked again, this time with the force of Devi's rise. Chase gripped the Witch's arm and stopped her from leaving.

"Let me go!" Devi commanded, her fingers curling around a growing glow. Chase tugged her closer, a tactic that would work if she meant to throw a punch, though it wouldn't do much against her spell.

"This is about both of us," he ground out. "And you just told me you don't know what to do about the Queen."

"My mother might!" Devi countered.

"You saw the Halfers go into the forest, Dev," Chase reminded her. "They're far closer than we are."

"She's your mother, too!"

The hissed words stayed tight within the group, though Chase looked across the Clubhouse to be certain no one was close enough to overhear. Ember's fingers spread against her thighs, tapping in rhythm. Her attention jumped between the Halfer and the Witch.

Devi blinked with awareness, her anger and the witchflame in her palm fading under the realization she'd blurted out a deep secret. Her cheeks flushed pink. She lifted her chin and squared her shoulders, daring the people around her to react. Ember would not take that challenge. Silence proved the others wise enough to leave it alone, as well.

"We need to go," Devi continued. "You're right, but it doesn't matter. We have to at least try to save the coven."

"And when we can't?" Chase asked.

"Then we think of something!" Devi insisted. "The Queen can't infect me. There must be something I can do."

Ember bit her bottom lip. Charlah couldn't take her, either, and the Queen hated her sparks. With a sigh, Ember shifted and made to move toward Devi. Nicu's heavy hand planted on her shoulder, careful to avoid skin contact.

"You are not going."

"Charlah talks to me," Ember countered.

"Nor you," Nicu charged Branna while ignoring Ember. "I can see your strain."

Branna narrowed her eyes, but nodded. "Apparently, I am not strong enough to take her, anyway," she conceded.

"Well, Nicu Coccia," Devi purred. "Are you offering your help? What would that cost?"

"Tell me," he spoke quietly, the price in his words. "Will Charlah be able to claim the Fae?"

"Not without the Witches," Devi whispered, eyes wide and mouth tight. "You're not coming with us."

"No," he agreed.

"To the Fae?" Branna demanded, her brow furrowed. "Can you not go to Edan, first? Not even now?"

Ember swallowed the lump in her throat and she shifted so Branna could not see her face. A mistake.

"What do you know about it?" Branna demanded.

"Enough," Nicu halted the question. "The Queen is on the move. We have our jobs."

"Okay, Fae. Be quick," Chase accepted with a wary nod. Then he whistled to grab Keegan's attention. "Lock up. Only open to Halfers."

Keegan blinked tired eyes and sent a quick wave from his deep seat in a faded armchair. Chase gestured Devi in front of him, directing her toward the hidden exit.

"Do not forget your true objective," Nicu ordered. The suspicion on Branna's face softened into fatigue. She nodded and Nicu trailed the half siblings.

Ember marked his movement through the Clubhouse, waited for the moment he would turn to her, give her a final order to obey, anger bubbling in anticipation.

Chase held the passageway open until Nicu passed. The Fae did not snap a parting threat, or glare at her in warning. He was eager to get to Center.

A torrid wave rushed Ember's head. She surged across the room. Her fingertips caught the crack of the hidden panel. She barely felt the pinching pain as she hauled open the door. Chase stood on the other side with blank features, Devi with a raised brow.

Nicu was already gone. Her chest tightened, breathing strained. She swallowed a lump of realization. Nicu bringing the Fae wasn't her greatest fear. That Nicu might choose the Fae terrified her.

Ember's top lip curled. She didn't need him to protect her freedom, to choose to keep her secret. She had herself for that.

"I'm coming."

"Nicu said—" Ember slashed her hand across Chase's words to cut him off.

"Nicu's gone. I'm sure not going to let him rule my life like he's been ruling yours."

Chase studied Ember for a long moment, turning the key around in his fingers. Branna appeared beside Ember, Susan towed along with stumbling steps.

"We will all go," Branna announced. Ember twisted toward her in surprise, having expected the Fae to want to drag her back to the table. "I can wrap us in shadows. Charlah won't realize we are coming."

"Are you sure?" Devi drawled. Branna's smile sharpened her mouth.

"You don't have a plan. Nicu does not have the right to bench me."

"I mean, you look a little fatigued." Devi's voice softened.

"If we're going to depend on you, I need to know you're capable. And drop the Fae parlay. I want real answers."

Branna snorted. "Visual illusions are as easy as breathing. Turning them physical takes a toll, but the effort brings nothing worse than a headache. Does that satisfy you?"

Devi strode into the tunnel, making room for the Fae. Branna pushed in to follow her, Susan's elbow in her grip as she tugged the older woman along. Ember slipped through last. Chase closed the door, then turned the key in the lock, leaving only one way out.

21

NICU

ocus. Control. Nothing wasted.

The freedom of movement. The crisp air behind Nicu's ribs. No one to wait for and no one to lead. He wanted to enjoy every moment, let his thoughts float in and away.

Instead, he planned his request.

The Fae would not approve. It was Nicu's job to keep them safe, to allow them to remain separate from the races trapped within Trifecta.

Would asking for their help be the correct choice?

Would assuming the Witches could take care of the Queen be more prudent?

What if the only other option was granting a wish?

This is the question that drove him, that directed his feet to Fae. The memory of wish-directed healing energy drew awareness to flesh that should carry a knife wound, yet moved as if never injured.

Nicu forced proper form, did not allow the question to tighten his fists or affect his stride. If he kept control of his body, perhaps it would be enough to regain control of the situation. Convince the Fae the right choice would be to act.

To rewrite fate.

Thwart chaos.

Surely the Fae would approve. Must approve.

Nicu struggled against the flow of thoughts, refused to give in to fears that they would deny his request, his warnings unheeded.

Focus.

Avoid that tangle of fallen branches. Adjust the path for minimal movement between giant trees, between him and his goal. He did not control the future. He controlled his steps.

Focus.

Don't think about the hybrid girl's touch, of the thoughts that flowed between them, the images he'd seen through her via Susan's mind. How his only thought had been to save Ember from the fog that threatened to pull her down with Susan.

Nicu ran to Center for help because in that moment of contact he admitted the truth. He would grant that wish if it meant saving her.

Doing so would seal him to a destiny he had not decided on.

A figure appeared in the space between two trees, yards ahead, seconds away from Nicu's full strides. Nicu tightened his core, widened his stance, and stopped.

The man's long coat hung close against his narrow frame, his height topping Nicu's. Elbows bent sharply at his sides, hands tucked into pockets at his waist, as if out for a lazy walk. A trilby hat rested on his head, holding back wavy auburn hair. Emerald eyes flashed with gem-tones.

A Wizard Nicu did not recognize.

Brandt's Wizard, who had dared put the Trimarked Child at risk.

Nicu shut out all thoughts of Fae and wishes in favor of being fully present. He readied himself for magic to be thrown his way. Eager for the moment he would turn the spell back on its master.

"I appreciate your caution," the man spoke across the ten feet of space Nicu held between them. "Though I suppose Fae aren't known for jumping to conclusions."

The Wizard stepped at an angle. Nicu moved in time, as if they walked opposite sides of a circle.

"Not that you're a normal Fae," the Wizard continued. "Something else I appreciate about you. Nevertheless, it's becoming something of a concern. But let's start out on equal footing. You're Nicu. I'm Tristan."

That the Wizard knew his name meant he'd been watched. Somehow, he had avoided the Witch and Fae looking for him, and gained intel in the process. Nicu maintained silence, waited for more to be revealed, refusing to give any of himself away. As their slow steps brought Nicu close to his path toward Center, he never considered turning his back to the intruder.

"Excellent choice," Tristan praised Nicu as if positioning him toward Center was a test. Irritation threatened to alter Nicu's thoughts. He breathed it out, let it go, ready for the next exchange.

"It's fine that you don't speak. Really, I prefer people who know how to listen, unlike that Brandt human."

Green eyes glinted, anticipating a response. Nicu retained his outward calm.

"Impressive. You certainly have perfected body control. I would venture to say you're the most adept at it of any Fae I've met. Including Wist."

Nicu's steps stopped three quarters through the revolution of the circle. Tristan paused as well, though Nicu could not tell whose feet had been first. He vowed to pay more attention.

"I assume Wist is who you were going to ask for help?"

This Wizard wanted to flaunt his knowledge. A different time, Nicu would discover how and why Tristan learned where

Nicu traveled. For now, he noted when grinding irritation replaced Tristan's oiled tone.

"You will waste your time. We both know the Elder will draw in the Fae, barricade your borders, and separate you from your precious Trimarked Child."

These were the thoughts Nicu had attempted to ignore on his rush through the trees. The fears he wouldn't voice, intent to control the present all the way into the future.

Would Wist keep Nicu from the hybrid girl? Would the Fae allow the Elder to? Protecting the Fae was paramount. They regarded the Trimarked Child's chaos as their greatest threat within Trifecta. That might change with news of the Queen. Nicu considered the future by assessing an example from the past.

When the barrier had been cut open, the Fae had not deemed it a personal risk. They did not ask Nicu to locate the intruder. He was sent out to look for signs of a repeat event. They had sent Terraborn Fae on patrols in human places of Trifecta where they were unlikely to run into anyone, particularly one of power who didn't wish to be found.

Nicu's lashes twitched, and he auto-corrected the flinch into a blink.

Tristan was likely correct. The council would seal the border despite the Laws of Convergence that governed how the races interacted within Trifecta.

But would they lock him in with them, leave the Trimarked Child unguarded with such a threat?

Debatable. Especially with Branna acting as guard, though they trusted the necromancer less than Nicu. It would depend on what they chose his greater purpose to be. And how much weight Wist's opinion held on the matter.

It was not a chance worth taking.

The Queen still needed to be neutralized. The need for a wish negated. The man before him might have answers. Nicu didn't doubt he had his own motives, and whatever truth he shared now did not mean he was honest. Nicu chose his words with that in mind.

"What is your purpose?"

"Such a large question coming from a Fae," Tristan commented, initiating their circular meandering once again. "Certainly one that has many answers. Which aspect are you interested in?"

Further proof Tristan knew much of the Fae. Nicu breathed out his disappointment that their conversation would not be simple. The realization was not a surprise, given the stranger's invocation of Wist. Knowledgeable or not, the Wizard was not Fae, an advantage for Nicu.

"Why did you stop me?"

"You assume that was on purpose," Tristan answered. "Why not consider it by chance?"

Nicu did not answer, preferring to interpret the question as rhetorical. There was strategy in the Wizard's speech. Tristan's lips tilted in an angled smile.

"I am interested in the guardian of the Trimarked Child, naturally."

Nicu was not satisfied.

"Why stop me?"

The Wizard's eyes narrowed with the repetition.

"Because the help you seek will lead to complications I am not prepared to deal with."

"Complications other than your kind being mind controlled?"

"The little damage that Charlah can do here is of limited concern. She cares for her family," his mouth twisted on the word. "She won't hurt them. I need her, though. I am certain Wist would close the borders if he knew about her. Unless, of course, you tell him she is interested in the Trimarked Child, which you will. You seem to have a deep need to keep her safe. Admirable. But as I need Charlah for my own purposes, that is not a scenario I can allow."

Tristan removed his hands from his pockets and spread his fingers. The cuffs of his coat retracted with the movement, revealing the white of his shirt, the gem-studded cufflinks now visible.

Nicu breathed deep into his nose, and concentrated on the structure of the Wizard's power. Tristan used his mage senses to tap into the DNA within the redwood beside him, extracting molecules of magic to Work them into his spell. Magic in Terra was more difficult to release, and the intruder's speed and skill suggested he'd lived in Terra longer than the five weeks he'd been in Trifecta. Nicu would consider it later, his current moment centered on his opponent. Tristan passed the gathered magic through his amethyst cufflink and directed a sleeping spell to form with his low chant.

It would fail once Nicu diverted the power. Though magic itself was invisible, Nicu's Fae senses allowed him to feel the flow of molecules, as he could discern the direction of the wind, or the location of the sun from the heat it radiated. Raw magic was difficult for him to mold. A completed spell was easier to manipulate, already tied at both ends by the original caster. Still, Nicu could not hold it.

He would need a sound strategy to defeat such a skilled mage. Using physical attacks might work, but would likely engage passive protective spells meant to react quickly. Too quickly for Nicu to redirect the power. The Work would not take long for the offensive spell, either, the chant simple. Cutting the distance between them shortened the time available for Nicu to capture and reWork the spell. He would stand his ground, then, and hope his particular skill was one the Wizard had not seen before.

The twist of magic flew at Nicu. Living Ink came to life, swirled across his body, and captured the molecules meant to harm him. He pooled the energy into his own hands. Nicu did not change the intent of the spell as he tore it from the Wizard's control and redirected the force toward its caster.

Tristan's hands fisted, pulled to the side. The energy flowed in reverse through Nicu, ripped from the grip of his tattoos and back into the Wizard's command.

Nicu found his center and regarded his opponent. He had not expected the Wizard's strength, but surprise had no place in Nicu's mind.

"Interesting," Tristan murmured, more intrigued than bewildered. He Worked strength and depth into the sleeping spell, intending to overpower Nicu with a jet of magic.

Tattoos flowed over dark skin, unhindered by the layers of clothing that protected Nicu from the autumn chill. Instead of catching the mass of magic, Nicu manipulated it while in flight, breaking it into smaller, physical hits, much like he would receive in the boxing ring at the training grounds in Center. He dodged most, and absorbed the few he could not deflect to store within his Ink.

The Wizard gathered more power as his previous spell dissipated, leveraging the air into his creation. A multi-roped binding spell flew toward Nicu. A blush of sweat coated his skin as he burst as many of the tentacles as possible, his tattoos snapping the hold of those that got through.

The next spell hit, this one petrifying Nicu's muscles. Nicu's tattoos expanded, the Ink flowed and shifted the energy into a brisk winter's chill. He gathered the Ink stored energy and thrust with a jab into the air, sending a force wave of power that kicked up forest debris in its path.

Tristan crossed his forearms just in time. Nicu's backlash activated Tristan's defensive shield. The wave broke apart, the only damage done was to the Wizard's hat as it flew from his head, freeing auburn waves to fall around his narrow cheeks.

"How very interesting." Tristan lowered his arms to reveal flushed skin and a mouth pursed in a sharp frown. "The taint of your power... transference from Ember. How did that happen? Who are you to my daughter?"

Nicu stopped breathing, stopped counting, stopped thinking, and stared at the Wizard.

Ember's father?

The Wizard took advantage.

He stepped once and closed the ten feet, appearing next to Nicu, shoulder to shoulder, facing opposite directions. Brilliant eyes flashed as he yanked Nicu to his side, one hand on the Fae's chest, and stepped again, directing Nicu onto the magical, fast moving path.

Nicu struggled to reorder his mind, to find focus in the blur of movement, regaining his control against the manipulations of the Wizard.

Before his long practiced skills could serve, Tristan bent his path. He increased their speed, and thrust Nicu's body into the unforgiving strength of an ancient redwood. Solid contact burst across the back of Nicu's head. Pain overtook his body and he sunk into darkness.

22

EMBER

*E*mptiness greeted the small group when they reached the edges of the Circle. Maintenance equipment was left abandoned wherever Work had been released. Ember questioned if Branna's shadowy shield was necessary until a stone rattled off to their left.

Branna lessened the shadows over her vision and located the Witch sitting in the tall sunflower stalks, their bright yellow petals following the sun as if it were midsummer instead of encroaching on winter. The sentry scanned the area, her attention slipping past their position, supporting the need for the illusion.

From that point forward, they guarded where they placed their own feet, careful to tread lightly so they didn't make the same mistake as the Witch. Hidden, but discoverable via sound.

They crept along the patterned cobblestone pathways that wandered through the entrance to the Circle, making their way toward the warehouses of a once busy industrial park that had packaged mountain runoff into plastic bottles. Past the renovated apartment buildings, sounds of movement whispered and clanged. Devi slowed her step, and the rest of the group followed.

Ember kept a close eye on her mother, aware that as they became closer to the Queen, her behavior might change. Touching Susan didn't send Ember back into her mind again without Nicu's catalytic touch. Susan remained calm and mobile with Branna's shadow mask held over her face, as if she was as malleable as a doll. She was trapped even further in her body than she'd ever been, buried under that fog Ember had seen. Ember's fingers tapped on her thighs, worried just how far away her real mom was.

Chase gripped Ember's arm and yanked her to the side. From a perpendicular path between the buildings, a few coven members stumbled deeper into the Circle toward the unaltered warehouses, pupils gleaming, their feet sure of their direction.

They'd been afflicted.

"Not a great time to let your mind wander," Chase whispered. Ember grit her teeth and gave a sharp nod. He was right. She'd insisted on coming, which was the reason Susan was being dragged by Branna. She needed to get her thoughts in order and focus.

The shadowed group reached the unfinished portion of the Circle. Stacks of debris littered the packed dirt paths cleared of concrete and pavement. Chase had pulled her behind one of the piles. Devi and Branna had also found places to hide, Susan safe at Branna's side. The narrow space wouldn't have been large enough for the Witches to pass without plowing into them, making their invisibility moot.

What in the verge had she been thinking, insisting on joining the team? So what if Charlah didn't like her sparks? What was that against an army of Halfer and Witch drones?

"We're screwed," Chase echoed her thoughts.

"Shut up," Devi hissed, running one hand over the bracelets on the opposite forearm. Her fingers danced without collecting, a sign she wasn't sure what to do, either. Once the wandering Witches and Wizards passed, Devi gestured everyone to follow her into the nearest warehouse.

They entered a side door of the old loading docks, the large roll-up truck entrances pulled closed. Retired forklifts and pallet jacks lined up against the outer wall. The rest of the room was empty except for the thick coat of dust and grime. Branna eased the shadows to check for hidden spies within the space, then dropped their camouflage and found a seat on a torn up, cushioned forklift chair.

Susan's binding remained in place. Unanchored to anything other than Branna's power, she stood still and silent.

"You're certain that blind is working?" Ember asked.

"Worried your sunshine friend is going to show up?" Branna demanded.

Susan released a muffled scream. Ember sped to her side even as Branna slid from her elevated seat. Susan bent backward, face tilted to the ceiling. Leona flickered into sight, arms around Susan as she lowered her to the ground.

"Mother," Devi gasped.

"I've been trailing you since you entered the Circle," Leona stated, easing Susan's head to the concrete floor.

"You saw through my shadows?" Branna asked.

"Are you surprised your Elders might have a few more tricks than expected?" Leona huffed. Her pointed glance toward Devi suggested her words weren't just for the Fae.

From a pocket in her skirt, Leona lifted out a small, black ring held by a loop of hemp rope. Her other hand passed a purple healing stone over the scratch Charlah had left on Susan's cheek. As the skin knit together, Leona murmured a lullaby sounding spell and lowered the ring until it hovered and spun centimeters from Susan's forehead.

A soft glow filled the hollow of the circle, growing in strength. Ember's eyes watered as she watched, refusing to take her attention from her mother and the Witch Working over her. The light grew with intensity and Ember narrowed her eyes against it until she was forced to squeeze them shut and look away, an arm raised to block its brilliance.

The flash dissipated, magic released. Leona sat on the floor with a sigh, pressing Susan's hair back as if soothing a child.

"You can remove the binding now," Leona informed Branna. The Fae studied Ember's mother for a moment, then flipped her hand as if dusting off a surface. The shadow blind drifted away.

Devi crossed her arms, lips pursed, and turned to Branna. "Is that light how you see her magic?"

"It isn't magic," Branna countered. "It's soul sharing."

"And now that we've freed one of her followers, the Queen will look for us," Leona warned. "We have to get moving. Chase, come carry Susan. I suspect she'll be sleeping for a while and we can't leave her here or she could be reclaimed."

Chase remained stationary, staring at the two women on the floor. His pockets bulged from clenched fists and his lips twisted with unspoken words. Ember's attention flashed between the High Priestess and the leader of the Halfers, seeing the strain of the years between them.

"Chase, please," Ember whispered, her hands trembling, no longer concerned about the cost, just needing her mother. "I can't leave her. I'll pay whatever —"

"Stop talking," Chase growled and strode forward. Despite his jerky motion and the dark scowl he directed toward Leona, he was gentle as he lifted Susan into his arms. "You need to get it into your head, Ember. This whole damn world owes you, not the other way around. Isn't that right, Mom?"

Leona paled with the announcement. Her amethyst eyes scanned the small group and registered the lack of surprise. She let out a slow breath in time with a shallow nod.

"I understand you are asking for a conversation, but we don't have time," Leona said. No one argued.

"Where should we go?" Devi asked. "It seems like the entire coven has been taken."

Leona shrugged. "I'm not sure. When the Queen came in, I ran to the archives and grabbed the ring." Leona moved to lift the artifact, then with a sharp glance toward Devi, dropped it into her pocket. Devi's heavy sigh suggested Leona had a habit of hiding interesting things from her daughter.

"Branna can tell where Charlah is," Ember offered, enjoying the Fae's glare.

Leona's attention jumped from Devi to Ember.

"How do you know her name?"

"She's been running around Trifecta all day," Branna replied with a smirk of retaliation. Her eyes had cleared of the protective shadow she'd taken to wearing. She shifted toward something on the outside. "Ember has become best friends with the Queen."

"How in the Convergence did she get into this realm?" Leona demanded.

"They have the starfall knife," Devi answered, her voice soft, eyes on her nails.

"They," Leona repeated, looking between Devi and Ember, Chase and Branna. "When this is over, there will be a lot to discuss. For now, we have to move. Branna, can you monitor the Queen from here?"

"She's approaching from the east, and not alone. They aren't moving quickly. That might be because there are a few of them close to us already."

"You can see all of them?" Leona asked.

"When I'm looking. She's sunlight, and they're starlight."

"Mom, where do we go?" Devi repeated.

"They're all around us? Are they in the building?" Leona asked Branna.

"Yes, and no," the Fae answered the questions in order.

"Obviously, you knew she was coming here, something else to talk about later. For now, what was your plan?" Leona asked Devi. Devi raised her gaze to her mother and shrugged.

"Typical," Leona murmured. Her hand slipped into the

pocket where she'd put the black ring, then she shook her head. "It may be too late to run. We'll have to make a stand. Why are each of you here?"

"Chase is here for the Halfers," Devi answered after a moment of silence. "The Queen is afraid of Branna."

"Maybe," Branna interrupted. "The hive members don't like my shadows, but can tolerate them. Charlah said my powers weren't fully awake. It took a magnification spell by Devi to trick her last time."

"And she can't afflict Branna, Ember, or me," Devi finished.

Ember gripped her hands behind her back and bit her tongue. She'd almost blurted out that Charlah didn't like her sparks, almost shared with the High Priestess that whatever power she had wasn't entirely contained by the Trimark tattoo. When Devi had inspected it last month, she'd mentioned there was evidence of a Witch's input with the pentacle. It made sense that the most powerful Witch in Trifecta may have had something to do with it, and wouldn't be happy to learn her Work didn't work.

Despite Charlah's danger, Ember wasn't prepared to reveal that secret, not if they could stop the Queen without it. Not when they were words she wouldn't be able to take back.

"Very well." Leona's voice deepened with the strength of decision. "Chase, take Susan into the building. Try to find an office or closet you can hide in. The three of you need to be caught," she directed to Devi, Branna, and Ember. "Keep the Queen distracted. I'll disappear to all eyes and sneak up on her. I can try to use the ring directly on the source and cut off her connection to the others."

"What is that ring, anyway?" Devi asked. The glint of interest followed her mother's motion as the older woman released the piece of jewelry from her pocket. Leona hesitated with her answer, the artifact always held by the hemp, rather than on its own.

"It's dragon bone," Leona answered. "The only one of its

kind. It was made so the Dragon Lord's mate would be safe from the dragon hive mind. That's why it may work on the Queen."

Leona disappeared and Devi sauntered toward the space where she'd stood, her arms stretched out, but not coming into contact with the body of her mother.

Devi huffed. "See her keep me out of the archives after this," she mumbled.

Branna directed the shadows to cover her eyes, a harbinger for the Queen. Ember threw her attention to the door a moment before someone banged against the metal. It flew inward to slam against the concrete wall. Aaron stepped in, followed by Charlah. Sunshine back-lit her entrance, setting her pale hair to shining, black eyes glowing with starlight.

23

EMBER

*E*mber studied each step Charlah took in case she picked up her speed, ignoring Aaron who stood between the Queen and the doorway. For the time being, Charlah appeared content with a normal pace, her bare feet silent against the concrete floor.

The female trio stood where Leona left them, halfway between the door to the outside and the raised loading platforms at the back, where Chase had disappeared with Susan. Devi and Branna stood on Ember's left. She glanced at them to check their reaction. Devi appeared bored. The necromancer's features displayed no more than her usual discontent. Ember breathed through her nose, tried to copy their unassuming demeanors. Her hands splayed against her jeans, pressing the cloth to hide the trembling in her body.

"I'm so glad you came to see me! You're so thoughtful, not making me chase you," Charlah chimed, her voice echoing off the concrete and metal surfaces in the cavernous garage.

A bodiless shadow flit across the light trail let in by the open door. At the same moment, Devi stiffened in defence and crossed her arms, fingers resting on her bracelets. Charlah's eyes narrowed on the movement.

"Why would you chase me?" Ember asked, drawing the Queen's attention.

"Oh, not you. Them." Charlah gestured toward the Witch and Fae.

"You said you had no use for me in your family," Devi charged.

"You're not for me. You're going to help my brother."

"Another came through with you?" Devi asked as she inched forward. Charlah frowned at the change. Aaron tilted his head as if listening to something. Charlah's eyes remained on Devi, her cheek turning toward Aaron as if deciding which one needed her full awareness.

"I want my knife," Devi demanded on another move forward, taking a forward point between Ember and Branna.

She'd seen the shadow, too, and used movement to pull Charlah's predator senses, to keep her away from whatever Leona tried to achieve. But if Leona was trying to free Aaron, wouldn't Charlah know through their connection?

Unless... Ember remembered her moments inside Susan's brain, how the cloud covered her mother's consciousness, how the Queen's thoughts floated above the fog. Charlah had said humans didn't make good family. Because they didn't integrate well? Aaron might have kept a part of himself away from the Queen, his mind much stronger than Susan's. If that was true, they needed a better distraction.

Ember stepped next to Devi.

"Charlah." The Queen fixed on Ember. Now what? She stumbled over the first question that came to her tongue. "Why isn't your brother part of your family?"

Charlah's brilliant grin accompanied a rapid clap.

"You ask the best questions. My brother was given a safeguard that doesn't let him be part of me. He's kind of like you. Nice, but not mine. Nice enough that he broke me out. But if he was mine, he would never feed me to that tree."

Ember scrambled her thoughts, hoped they'd fall into a

pattern. She had the most information. She should be able to figure this out. Her gaze fell, her attention caught by the star-fall knife. A weapon she must have gotten from Brandt's Wizard.

Ember's breath left her lungs, images forming into an answer before she had the words.

"Your brother is the man who was looking for you, isn't it?"

"Mm-hmm," Charlah agreed, her reply easy. The topic hadn't been enough to distract her. Ember, on the other hand, stood frozen. Her eyes stuck on the Queen's white hair, the lift of her cheek, and pointed chin. Tristan's sister. The most they shared as siblings was their narrow length. The shape of her nose, however, seemed to have passed down to Ember.

This crazy witch was her aunt? Ember swallowed down a gag, looked away. She didn't want to discover any other similarities, physical or otherwise. She focused on Aaron, wanting to check on him. The movement of her gaze inadvertently drew Charlah's attention to the human.

Well, crap.

Branna's shadows sped across the floor. Her lips tightened into an open scowl, her white teeth a stark contrast to her dark eyes. Charlah squared her body against Branna's, her arms swept outward, fingers crowned with jagged nails flared, palms out. The shadows burst into feather-shaped shrapnel that reversed course. Branna lifted her chin and called forth her tattoos, the Ink spreading, shifting to catch and collect the projectiles. Branna flinched when a few feathers contacted skin, thin lines of blood marking wherever they penetrated.

Charlah spun with a throaty grunt. Aaron's brow angled, lips parted with unspoken questions, his eyes flitting between Charlah who was close, and Ember who remained across the room, as if he wasn't certain which one to ask. Ember opened her mouth to call his name, to catch his awareness and keep it.

Too late. Charlah's hand flew past him to claw at the air.

Leona appeared in the space behind Aaron, her lips drawn apart against the grip Charlah had in her orange-red hair.

"You think you can steal more of my family, you hag?"

Leona twisted, reached across her body, the black circlet on its hemp chain directed toward Charlah.

Devi's body stiffened, her fists clenched. The Witch glared toward Charlah's attack on her mother with frosty green eyes, clearly wanting to help. Ember rushed to her side, a soft brush of shoulder to shoulder. She wouldn't be able to stop Devi if she truly wanted to go to her mom, but the contact would help the Witch focus. Of all of them, Leona had the best chance. Devi had to know that, too, since she stayed put. Just as Ember hoped.

The Queen screeched in rage. She yanked Leona's hair to wrench her neck downward. Aaron captured the Witch's arm. The High Priestess let out a pained grunt as he angled the limb up, keeping the ring spaced between himself and the Queen.

Aaron's movements were so in tune with Charlah, with no lag time. After her dive into Susan's mind, Ember had thought the connection was a broadcast system, the drones forced to do her bidding, but it was worse. The people inside the bodies were truly buried under the Queen's fog. The hive mind was her mind.

Ember's fingers tapped against her thighs, ran the number of mixed-blood Halfers, knowing there were hundreds more Witches and Wizards, many of them under the Queen's control. What was Charlah that made it possible to spread herself among all these bodies and only get stronger?

An experiment, she'd said earlier in the day. An experiment gone wrong. Like aunt, like niece.

Was this what Ember would become? A power so big and explosive it would drive her crazy?

Not today. Today, Ember was whole. She could help. Leona thought the artifact was the key, so she would start there.

"Do you want me to get the ring?" Ember asked, her voice raspy and thick.

Charlah clicked her tongue and hummed. The Queen's thoughts darkened her features. One of the enemy had snuck up on her. She wouldn't be as quick to trust the girl who stood with the opposition.

The sectional doors where semi-trucks once parked their trailers opened with a rusty squeal. Ember faced the noise, watched as two of the hive hopped to the lower floor, ignoring the steps. Branna and Devi faced the threat, Devi fingering stones and Branna balling her fists.

No one came forward for Ember. The Queen waited for her reaction. This was a test.

"Don't fight." Ember's breath struggled through the warbled constrictions of her throat. Branna ignored her, wide-eyed attention on the Wizard stalking her. Devi sent her a narrow glare, then sighed and dropped her arms. The Halfer hooked his fingers into Devi's thick bun, wrapping his second arm around her shoulders and upper chest. Devi glared at Charlah as she attempted to shake free, but her captor did not budge.

"Branna." Ember tried to copy Nicu's tone, failing when her voice broke. Clearing her throat, she tried again. "Branna, stand down. You cannot beat the Queen."

Then Ember opened her lips and breathed through the formations, words softer than a whisper. "I need to get the ring."

Branna's grumble vibrated from behind her ribs. She lowered her fists, and the afflicted Wizard grabbed her wrists to pin at her back. His other forearm ground against her neck and jaw. Branna's mauve eyes darkened to a deep plum. Her tattoos snapped and shifted, but they did not bother the Wizard.

Ember took a deep breath, settled her shoulders, and

turned to greet Charlah's sparkling eyes. Ember had satisfied the Queen.

"Step carefully," Charlah guided. "And you two had better not move." A snide comment for Devi and Branna.

Ember studied Aaron as she closed the distance, trying to see if she could find that part of him he held away from Charlah. His irises were the same deep blue, but the pupil was foggy, contaminated by the Queen's light.

Leona's teeth ground together when Aaron forced her to move, to provide Ember ease of access. Charlah smiled at Ember's calm procession, as if at a young child who deserved praise for following instructions.

"Go ahead," Charlah encouraged. Ember focused on the dark, hollow disk that floated in the air. She reached for the matte black ring, gasped when it moved from her on its own, repelled by her fingers. Charlah chuckled. "You can't touch it, silly. It's made for one person only. Grab the cord."

"Why not?" Ember asked. A curious tickle entered her brain, and she approached the artifact again, just to watch it arc away.

"It was created by a fate-mage," Charlah snapped. "Now stop playing and get it from that hag!"

Ember collected the hemp rope. Leona's grip tightened and Ember met her focused gaze, filled with an urgent message Ember couldn't hope to understand. Wouldn't the Priestess prefer the artifact in Ember's hands than the Queen's?

With a firm tug, Ember snatched the ring from Leona. A low buzz vibrated within Ember's gut. Nausea struck her dizzy, and electricity buzzed beneath her skin.

Ember gaped at Leona. Her attention flickered to Aaron, then Charlah.

This was a mistake. The High Priestess couldn't see Ember spark, couldn't know the Trimark tattoo didn't contain whatever power lived in her blood.

Aaron twisted Leona's arm behind her body, holding the

High Priestess's bracelets away from her fingers. Charlah's lips curled into a wicked smile as she drew a fingernail across Leona's cheek.

"No!" Devi's voice dropped into an octave full of rage. Ember heard the sounds of her struggle, swallowing the guilty relief that Leona's enslaved mind might not recognize if Ember's power flared.

Leona's sneer negated the need for either Ember's or Devi's response.

"I have guarded against you, Queen," the High Priestess declared. Charlah tilted her head, curiosity puckering her lips.

"Are you one of the ten that made me?"

"My mother," Leona admitted, dark shame on her cheekbones.

"Did you help make her?" Charlah gestured to Ember, who inched away, not wanting the High Priestess's scrutiny.

"I did not," Leona hissed. Ember flinched at the vehemence in the High Priestess's voice. Though their interactions had been rare, she'd always treated Ember with tolerance. A mask that hid her darker feelings, apparently.

The Queen lifted a finger to her own lips in response to Leona's answer and leaned forward. "Are you the one who bound her?"

Devi's muffled shout suggested her captor had gagged her.

Ember didn't dare look, keeping her focus on the hypnotic sway of the ring, trying to breathe. Charlah's accusation sent lighting coursing through her veins, carving heated anger into her nerves. A single spark bit into the air, and a fine mesh crystallized across her skin.

Knowing if Leona bound her wouldn't change anything. It would change everything if Ember was exposed to the coven.

This was because of the stupid ring and her brilliant idea to use it, only to find out she couldn't control it.

Maybe she didn't have to control it to use it. Manipulate

the situation and convince Leona the blue energy came from the artifact.

Her heart pounded in her chest, fully aware of the risk she took, knowing this was her only chance. She gathered the length of the cord in her fist to close the distance. The small circle tried to pull away, limited by the hemp. Ember intentionally thought of her shield. Blue light flickered over her skin and solidified. The circlet stopped struggling when sparks danced across its matte surface.

"Don't touch it!"

Leona. Charlah. One or both. Ember couldn't tell with the rush of power in her ears. A flush of triumph warmed her, a certainty that if they were yelling about the ring, they must think the magic came from her attempt to grab it. Not from her at all.

Ember closed the last few millimeters, the whole process only a couple of heartbeats long. The blue shell on her skin made contact with the circle of dragon bone.

Pain burst from the center of Ember's chest, torn from her heart. She cried out, her energy pulled from her by something beyond herself, outside this space and time. A demand for safety and freedom.

The ring disappeared as she fell and took her consciousness with it.

24

AARON

S parks of Ember's power burst through the room with the ring's disappearance. Blue flashes filled Aaron's sight, burned into his mind and fought back the fog, cutting through the link between him and the hive.

Charlah's mental grip reached for him, trying to cement her control. She was desperate to search his memories and explore the flash of recognition he had regarding the ricochet of energy. But it was too late. He was free.

Charlah's scream split his eardrums, anchoring him to his body. Aaron blinked through the numb aftermath. Thoughts scrambled, he stumbled back and drew Leona with him.

Aaron swallowed a thick lump of guilt and tried to tug Leona behind him, to make up for when he hadn't been in control. She jerked her elbow from his grasp and stepped in front of him, blocking his attempts. Aaron's brain caught up with her actions and he dropped his hands, happy to have the Witch in the position of protector.

A soothing quiet filled Aaron's thoughts with the removal of the hive mind, yet the harsh silence in the room sent goosebumps across his skin. He peeked around Leona. Charlah stood over Ember's prone body. His legs moved, propelled him into the arm Leona snapped out to keep him back.

Right. He was vulnerable. Leona was not. As much as he wanted to get to Ember, he needed to stay far away from the hive mind.

"Where did it go?" Leona hissed. She squinted at Devi. The younger Witch was no longer captured, but stood protectively over the unconscious body of her previous captor, her brilliant cranberry hair a flame that helped deepen the darkness of Branna, though perhaps the Fae's shadows were at play. Leona stared hard in their direction for a moment. Seemingly satisfied, she turned back to the stationary Queen, who was attached to Ember's side.

"Aaron," Charlah called sweetly, as if they were friends, as if she hadn't ripped his world apart in a matter of hours. Being a drone had been bad enough, but it wasn't the worst part.

Brandt.

Pain flashed along with the thought of his friend. He shoved it away to deal with later. If there was a later.

"The entire family is gone, Aaron. Did Ember do this on purpose, or was it the ring?"

Black eyes rose to find him peering over Leona's head.

"Don't answer," Leona warned, but Aaron couldn't stay silent. Charlah's heart beat fiercely for her family.

Fiercely, as in willing to do anything. Memories emerged from where Charlah had tried to hide them. Images of the Queen's hand around a girl's neck, feet lifted from the floor. Curiosity ablaze while she watched the struggling Halfer fade away just because the human dared to talk to one of her new family about escaping.

Charlah couldn't believe Ember might betray her.

"She's clueless about magic," Aaron offered, echoing words he'd heard in the hive. Charlah smiled, held out her hand.

"You miss being family, don't you? Come back, Aaron. I can fix this. We'll get everyone back, you'll see."

Aaron stiffened, knew refusing would add to her anger, but desperate to keep his mind his own.

The hive mind gave Aaron an up close view of magic. How it was harvested from Nature, then tangled into something new through strength of will. It was a perspective his humanity slipped around and through, seeing without comprehending.

Susan couldn't float as he had. Instead, the magic found the cracks in her mind, oozed within and expanded the space between what made her human. Charlah used the magical energy like glue, holding Susan together. Though this helped stabilize their connection, even the increase of the Halfer's voices didn't drown out Susan's mental screams.

The Halfers were better at ignoring it, somehow primed for the magic that wrapped around them in a cozy cocoon, immersing them in the hive. Charlah had felt confident in their captivity, satisfied when they compacted under the force of her will. Their true selves slept, and their bodies were hers to use.

The Witch minds acclimated like fish to water, sinking in and under, drowned in the Queen's power. They were her natural prey, she the perfect predator.

Aaron's thoughts had never been far from the surface. He hadn't wanted to drown in the hive. Desire had been enough, and he'd stayed afloat. For that reason, Charlah had kept him close. She wouldn't let him go, either. Despite the effort it took her to keep his presence in her hive, Aaron's unique collection of memories had proven valuable.

Whatever Ember had done with the ring had broken Charlah's hold, freeing the whole of her family. He would not willingly return.

"Come," Charlah purred.

Leona stretched as far as her height allowed, arms angled out to stop him if he tried. Aaron curled his shoulders forward, hands tucked in his coat pockets as he shrank behind the Witch.

No shame in knowing your limitations.

The Queen gave up on enticing Aaron and stared at the girl on the ground. Confusion waged war with rage across Charlah's pale features.

"I don't understand. Ember knew I needed a family. Why would she take it away from me? Or was it an accident?" Galaxies burned, her hot glare reaching Aaron once more. "Tell me. Tell me if she meant it."

Leona tried to shift and block Charlah's line of sight. Whether it was her magic or residue of the hive mind, the Queen held his stare, but she couldn't make him speak. He said nothing, not wanting to add fire to the rage. Not wanting to see the result.

Charlah's top lip twitched, arched up into a sneer. Her lashes lowered, attention once more on the girl at her feet.

"Well. She cost me my family either way, didn't she? The Witch and the necromancer, too." Each syllable dropped deeper into menace. The calm Charlah had been projecting dissolving into her acidic words. "So. I guess she'll just have to take my place, instead."

The tree rose front and center in Aaron's mind. The bark twisted as if alive, parting into a black hole.

"No!" He moved around Leona, used his size and strength to overcome the High Priestess this time.

Charlah pouted and looked through her lashes at him.

"That's not very kind of you," she argued.

"N-no. Think about it. Brandt and Ember hate each other." Leona stiffened with the mention of Brandt's name and Aaron felt the heat of her gaze at his back.

"It isn't like they'll be having tea parties," Charlah spat.

Aaron stumbled forward, slipped from Leona's grip and fell to his knees in the spot Ember's body had been a moment before, gone along with the Queen who took her.

"Verge," Leona hissed behind him. Footsteps echoed through the hollow space as everyone approached where

Aaron knelt. "We'll have to regroup. At least she doesn't have her family."

"We have to get to No Man's Land," Aaron interrupted, hands gripping his hair, pulling hard at the roots. He struggled to stand. His attention flickered across the faces in front of him, his heart pounding with such strength he had to swallow the urge to be sick.

"We lost the ring," Leona argued. "It was our only hope against her hive mind."

"She's going to feed Ember to that fading tree!" Aaron shouted. His voice filled the warehouse with the force of his panic, the tight desperation of need.

"Trees don't eat people," Chase muttered, leading Susan from their hiding place. The woman trembled, her stormy eyes focused on Aaron.

"You can't let her," Ember's mom commanded, skeletal fingers reaching for Aaron. "You can't let her do that to my baby."

"What does that mean, feeding a tree?" Devi demanded in a huff. "Is it some secret hive mind thing?"

"The tree eats souls," Aaron answered. "Brandt's soul, first."

"And it's in No Man's Land." Devi spoke as if she were collecting an interesting fact. Her eyes widened, lips dropped open. Aaron didn't have time for her personal revelations.

"Whoever her brother is, he's trying to grow it with more," he continued. "It's why he wanted her, and the way Charlah moves... we're already too late."

"Like hell," Leona announced. She pulled purple, gold, smokey gray and milky white stones, piled them in her palms, and walked until they bathed in the sunlight.

"Devi," the High Priestess commanded and Devi stood by her mother's side, her hands cupped beneath the ones cradling the gems. "Lock us down."

Devi closed her eyes.

Wind twisted around the Witches' feet, burst through the

room, rattled the very foundation of the building. It exploded with the demand of magic, leaving the structure intact despite the pressure. Outside, the windstorm howled with the force of an oncoming freight train. A flash of colorless bright light filled the sky, infiltrated the warehouse and blinded them all.

Sobs echoed through the loading dock in the aftermath. Aaron blinked toward the sound, and found Susan's body tucked under Chase's shoulder, her tremors shaking them both. The Halfer focused on his pure blood family, his lips flat even though his lids lowered with reluctant respect.

"What happened?" Aaron asked.

"They threw up a shield," Branna answered when no one else had, standing as separate as Aaron. Her deep mauve eyes found his. "How fast is she?"

Aaron shrugged, hands out and empty. The Fae huffed, dismissing him as useless. Aaron tried not to take offense, recognizing his lack of knowledge was not helpful. Branna searched for a beacon only she could see, her lips flat. A trembling finger rose, indicating No Man's Land.

No. She couldn't have made it.

Devi's movement directed Aaron toward the door. He followed her out even as Leona gripped her daughter, abandoned gems scattering on the broken concrete outside the warehouse.

"Where are you going?" Leona demanded as Devi turned east, the opposite direction Branna pointed.

"No matter what the Queen does now, we don't have a way to stop her," Devi stated as she ripped her arm away from the High Priestess. "I know a place where I might get answers."

Leona stared after her daughter, took a deep breath, then set to follow. Devi flashed an annoyed glance at her mother, but if she said anything to the High Priestess, Aaron didn't hear it over the pounding of his own feet headed toward No Man's Land.

25

EMBER

he wind beat against Ember's face, moving so quickly it was hard to inhale. She woke with a gasp, instantly nauseous with the blur of movement surrounding her. She focused on the face so near her own and no longer felt the need to breathe over the desire to escape, pushing against the thin arms that cradled her.

"Oh, you're awake," Charlah said. Her hold on Ember didn't falter despite Ember's struggles.

"You were very naughty, Ember," the Queen chastened. "You know how much I needed a family, and you took it away."

Fades. Charlah hadn't bought that the explosion came from the ring, and apparently, her power plus the artifact had stripped Charlah of the only thing she cared about. Ember gasped against thin air, tried to look around, but closed her eyes as bile rose. She'd never moved so swiftly in her life. Hadn't even been in one of the electric cars kept for the humans of Trifecta. Speed was not a pleasant experience.

"It was an accident," Ember tried.

"I'm certain it was," Charlah agreed. "But I'm also convinced you would have done it, anyway, just to save them."

Ember froze, looking at Charlah with her mouth agape. Is that what she would have done? Save the Halfers who made her life so uncomfortable? Chosen to rescue Aaron, yes, but the rest?

"I'm not sure," Ember said the truth aloud. Charlah frowned, then her features drooped.

"Oh, now you're making me sad about what I have to do. Stop it."

The wind stripped Ember's fear-dried throat, and she coughed into Charlah's shoulder.

"Do what?"

"Feed you to the tree in my place."

Ember didn't understand how a tree could be fed a person. She did know something that was eaten was generally dead. She pressed against Charlah again, knowing it was pointless, needing to fight, anyway. Charlah tightened her grip, fingers and arms becoming bands around Ember's much weaker body.

She had other choices. Ember took a deep breath and closed her eyes, searched into the places where her power lived, where it would buzz and nip at her insides whenever it was tired of confinement.

A low warmth met her, but no surge.

She was drained.

That fading ring! Her power had been stolen, used to send that ring to safety. Ember would not have made that decision. The artifact was the only thing Charlah feared. She'd just wanted to keep her secret from the High Priestess.

Now she had no power at all.

Fine. She'd have to wait, hoping her energy rebuilt itself so she could use it to nip at the Queen, keeping her at a distance. She might have a chance to run. From a super strong Witchy Queen who moved faster than vision could follow. No big deal.

When it was fight or die, the answer was usually simple. The means, on the other hand, a fading mess.

The wind around Ember paused, then withdrew. Ember

gasped in the vacuum. Her lungs seized. She coughed up precious oxygen, fingers biting into where she gripped Charlah.

Was this the Queen? How the verge was Ember going to fight magical suffocation?

Air returned, but from behind them, chasing the Queen with a roar. Ember pressed her hands over her ears as the gale whipped around and past, bringing with it the sharp sting of pine needles and debris that pelted her through her clothes. It stopped in a wave before them, dissolving into a vertical, shimmering mist. Charlah slowed to a halt and watched as the moisture evaporated into nothingness.

Charlah toed the air, the ball of her foot flattening as if pressed against the outer barrier. Ember's brow wrinkled, and she opened her senses. Veil energy reverberated from the dome high above. She felt nothing from this invisible fence, couldn't figure out what it looked like, but it trapped Charlah.

Ember timidly moved her outer arm forward, encountering the same, solid force that did not allow her to pass. The power did not react to her. The energy inside did not spark in assonance. This was not the Veil.

Had Leona created this boundary? Was she working out a new plan to capture the Queen? Ember thought about the dagger, tucked into Charlah's belt, close to Ember's ribcage where she was held crossways to the Queen. Could she get it? Would it help her, at least delay Charlah until help could come?

Charlah hissed and ducked behind a boulder, sending whiplash down Ember's spine. While Charlah peeked around the stone, Ember struggled with the Queen's iron grip, stopping when she heard an odd scraping sound approaching the clearing from the other side. She leaned with Charlah to investigate.

Tristan dragged someone through the leaves in No Man's Land, solidifying the theory that this new barrier was Witch-made, probably around Witch-land. Tristan used his path to slide the body he hauled against an impossible tree at its center. Charlah's tree. Or Tristan's. The one that ate people.

The one Nicu Coccia pressed against.

Ember's heart threatened to fail under the assault of her fear. Nicu's chin fell to his chest, his locs spread in disarray around his shoulders. Inactive. She opened her mouth to call to him, but even if he woke up, he wouldn't be able to get through this barrier that was not Trifecta's barrier.

Charlah dropped Ember's feet to the ground, gripped her wrist, and turned to run in the opposite direction before Ember gained her balance. Her steps staggered as Charlah dragged her. The Queen used her strength and momentum to hold Ember until her legs were under her again.

"Is he going to feed Nicu to the tree?" Ember gulped.

"He needs something of Fae. Whether it's that boy?" Charlah shrugged.

Ember fell to her knees and threw up. Charlah caught Ember's hair and held it back.

"Shh," the Queen soothed. "It can be painless, as long as that fate-mage didn't anger Tristan."

Ember grit her teeth, a raw chuckle cutting her throat. All Nicu did was make people angry.

He was Fae. The strongest person she knew. And if he died, she'd cut down that damn tree and make him, and it, pay for not keeping his promise. For leaving her without her anchor.

"Come on," Charlah urged when Ember's heaving stopped. The Queen's voice chimed a Witch's chant through the forest. Birds answered her back. Ember flinched from the spell, then blinked as she realized the sour taste of vomit left her mouth. Her skin tingled, and she lifted her hands to find the dirt falling away into dust. "There. All better."

As if a bit of magical refreshing was all Ember needed, Charlah gripped Ember's arm and continued their march.

They weren't moving as fast as before. Though they still sped through the forest on Charlah's magic path, the Queen had slowed her steps to match Ember's stride. Charlah cut a path through the Witch's territory, close enough to the Fae border that Ember saw the clash of hibernating vines that marked the separate Witch and Fae territories.

"Charlah, I cannot go onto Fae land."

The Queen snorted and threw a sharp look over her shoulder. "Are you lying now? I've been through many times and the silly fate-mages never even noticed." Charlah dragged Ember closer to prove her point.

"I am forbidden to cross the border!" Ember gasped, digging her heels in and clawing at Charlah's hand. The Queen redirected her path, keeping Ember on pace with pure strength.

"Oh, I see. Well, don't worry. We're not going there, anyway. Since I can't feed you to the tree, and I don't want to be fed to the tree, I'll have to do the worst thing ever," she scowled. "Go back to Heldu."

"The Witch realm?" Ember exclaimed, her body moving in automatic motions.

"Yep. The knife is out of magic, but it doesn't matter because I have you," her twinkling voice sang.

"What do you think I can do?"

"Use your power to part the Veil."

"I open holes to the outside, but only for a short time. I can't get you to a different realm," Ember stuttered, the words far too similar to what she'd said to Brandt.

"Stop lying," Charlah snapped. "Aaron told me you manipulate its power. Family doesn't have secrets."

Ember's lids flickered over paraded images. Being pressed against the barrier, a blade to her throat. The world shattering into shades of blue. Electricity raging through her body, tearing her apart, holding her together. And Nicu, there to save her.

Not this time.

Ember swallowed, painfully aware of her empty pockets. She looked around for forest provided weapons, and landed on the starfall knife tucked into Charlah's belt. Her breath stuttered in her lungs. It was on the opposite side of the Queen's body. She wouldn't be able to reach without giving herself away. Ember would have to be patient, wait for her chance. If one came, she'd be ready.

The static sound of rushing water marked their arrival at the Pine River. Charlah showed no signs of slowing, though the forest floor dropped toward the low river. Ember tried to drag her step. The Queen didn't hesitate when she stepped over the raised edge. Ember screamed in surprise. Pulled over the drop, her legs buckled underneath her and she landed in the thin stretch of mud between the earthen bank and the river's flow, undoing much of Charlah's cleaning spell.

"You aren't hurt." Charlah gripped under Ember's arm and hauled her to her feet.

"My knees," she tried to protest, but Charlah only frowned.

"They still work. Let's go. Then you can stop lying and I can leave."

"I'm not lying," Ember stressed, her brain fumbling with ideas, trying to get a grip on one. Sending Charlah out to afflict more innocent people squeezed Ember's heart. She didn't want to do it. Leona seemed to know a lot about the Queen, enough that she hadn't been frightened. She'd had a plan that neutralized the Queen. They could find a different way to get it to work.

"Charlah, I don't want you to go." Ember rushed through the words, hoped they sounded desperate instead of deceitful. The Queen brightened at the declaration.

"Maybe I misjudged you. Maybe you just didn't understand," Charlah presumed. With a happy shrug, she forced Ember to continue through the mud. "Okay, you can come with me."

Wait. That's not what she meant.

She couldn't go to Heldu. She had to pay back Chase, especially knowing the Fae weren't after her. Yet. And she had to stay behind to take care of her mom, to make the deals and take advantage of Aaron's goodness in order to make sure Susan was safe. She needed to know what happened to Nicu.

Ember gasped at the flood of connections, the number of reasons to stay overwhelming and unexpected. She hadn't thought anything tied her to this place, had believed that she was trapped more than anyone else.

Charlah tugged Ember to the steep angle of the high bank and parted a plant life curtain to expose an opening in the vertical rise.

"This is where Tristan brought me in. It's just a dirty hole, but it leads to the most powerful place."

"We're not going to the barrier?" Ember asked, peering into the earthen path.

"Oh," Charlah sniffed. "No, there are too many humans on Terra. Besides, I've decided that I'll get back at those Witches who didn't want me. And if I'm super sneaky, they won't realize my brother broke me out and I can collect a new family. An earth-mage only family."

Charlah's dreamy sigh was Ember's nightmare. The Queen was determined. Desperate.

"And you get to come with me!" Charlah exclaimed as if that were the best part of the plan. "Isn't this so much better than going into that tree?"

Then she pulled Ember into the dark tunnel.

26

NICU

*B*ark bit into Nicu's back, the pressure increasing as his consciousness revived. Had the Wizard left him where he fell?

But no. The energy was not Terra's. Each section of Trifecta held the essence of the inhabitants' realms. Fae magic settled in lines that mimicked the structure of its material. Witch magic flowed like blood. Terran magic buried into the core of things, making it difficult to access.

Here, stagnation reigned. At Trifecta's center, the powers of the realms repelled each other, creating a triangular space without magic or life.

Nicu opened his eyes. Confusion increased the ache in his head as he drew mental measurements. The edges of No Man's Land were wrong, too close to his extended legs for him to be pressed against a tree at its border.

Someone had grown a tree within No Man's Land. An impossible feat conquered in weeks, and this was no sapling. Nicu studied the pine bows that started a foot above his head, the branches thicker than a redwood of the same age. The small needles overlapped each other, where a redwood's spread out in bursts. This was unlike the pines growing in and around Trifecta.

Yet, none of that told him why, or how, it existed.

"It's a giant sequoia."

Tristan stood to Nicu's left, his hat in his hand as he studied the height of the pine. "Terra varieties don't grow taller than their redwood cousins, but this one is Helduan. All it needs is a bit more sustenance, and we shall strike the sky," he said with an angled smile.

Nicu's mind drew a painful blank that had nothing to do with his head wound. What would a Wizard need with a tree? Wrong question. What did this Wizard need with this Helduan tree?

Nicu took inventory of his own body, which seemed mostly sound, but not fully functional. The tender bump at the back of his head was troublesome. If he tried to rise, the pain would incapacitate him for a time. His vision would blur, possibly fade completely. He might fall, leaving the possibility of combat out as well. Even if at his peak, running away wasn't an option with the Wizard's abilities.

There was nothing left for it. Nicu would have to speak.

"The cost of its existence must be high," he offered to Tristan.

The Wizard's lips angled down. He raised the hat to his uplifted face, slid it along the tilt of his head to capture and hold his hair in place, away from eyes that lowered to Nicu.

"Careful that you don't become more bothersome than you're worth. I've noted you are tenacious toward your goals and I need to convince you not to go to Center. I brought you here to observe my proof." Nicu didn't respond to the bait. Tristan's eyes narrowed to sharp slits. "About Wist, of course. Do you think he isn't aware of this? That he doesn't have a hand in why you don't?"

Nicu shifted slowly, monitoring the depth of vertigo the

movement created as he organized his thoughts. Tristan could not be trusted. He would use the truth for his benefit. Nicu's latest task kept him far from the center of the dome. Ordered to pass over the watch of the hybrid girl, who was often near No Man's.

Tristan had already convinced Nicu he was familiar enough with the Elder to understand his motivations. That Wist's name was the only one Tristan invoked suggested the Elder bypassed the council. It was within character, as Wist's recent conversations with Nicu had been of his own accord, rather than as a speaker for the Elders. The holes baked into the logic left Wist's involvement questionable, another point in the Wizard's favor. Wist would ensure he was not suspected. This time, the truth suited Tristan's needs. Wist had kept Nicu from discovering an impossible tree.

Tension spread from Nicu's shoulders to his spine. He'd been caught unprepared. That his situation had been manipulated to keep him that way did not satisfy. Something burned behind Nicu's eyes, something that felt like anger toward the Fae.

Emotions bubbled, threatened to overcome his thoughts. Nicu refused to give them space, or to allow even a twitch of his eyebrows to give them away. He had no doubt every word Tristan chose was meant to inspire this internal battle. He would not allow the Wizard to win.

No matter the complete truth, Nicu would discover it later. He shut down a thought before it manifested, an image that he might not leave No Man's. Such thoughts were dead ends, and dead ends did not allow for him to keep his High Magic bound promise to the hybrid girl.

This Wizard would not force him to be forsworn. Neither would the Elder, if Tristan's warning proved truthful.

"How long have you known Wist?" Nicu asked. An offer of his own bait. Blood darkened the Wizard's skin, confirming there was more to this story.

"Longer than I wished to," Tristan clipped each word against sharp teeth. Nicu planned his next words to draw more from the Wizard.

His plan fell apart. Tristan spun with barely a flare of his long coat, the tails remaining as straight and structured as their owner. A thunderous noise crashed through the forest, and could only belong to a human. Aaron Harwell, running into No Man's. Fated power tightened in the air around Nicu.

Aaron's eyes were wide and wild as he searched the clearing, not finding what he wanted. He stumbled back when he saw Nicu against the tree and Tristan standing tall beyond him.

"Who trapped who?" Aaron asked, then winced as if he hadn't meant to speak aloud. Proving he no longer belonged to the Queen.

Nicu hid the upward twitch of his lips by lowering his chin, pulling air through his nose, deep into his lungs to ease the bands around his chest.

"She isn't here," Aaron wheezed. The human's skin became patchy with the contrast of pale fear and damp from exertion. Nicu improved his posture, shifted in his seat and judged the light blur of his eyes as a satisfactory improvement. He anticipated needing to move soon. There was only one person Aaron could mean.

"And who would you be looking for?" Tristan drawled. Aaron glanced toward the Wizard dismissively. Stopped. His eyes connected the tree, Nicu resting against it, and the tall stranger.

Aaron's face flushed crimson, and he squared his body to Tristan.

"Out on another social call?" he demanded through clenched teeth. "Asking about more lost kids?"

Nicu stilled, waited to see what this confrontation revealed. Aaron provided a distraction, but escape was still impossible. He sat within line of sight of both upright figures, and Aaron's well-intentioned attack against a powerful Wizard might require Nicu to intercede.

Tristan extended his arms, white cuffs peeked from his coat. He held his tongue for now, though. Nicu watched Aaron's eyes flicker between the Wizard and Fae, battling between priorities. He strode to Nicu's side and squatted, making the correct choice.

"You okay? The Queen was bringing Ember here."

"What?" Tristan's voice blasted through the clearing. Whatever intention he had for Nicu trampled beneath the emotions brought on by Aaron's announcement. "Where are they coming from?"

"The Circle," Aaron answered, his surprise getting the best of him as he shared information without thought. Nicu's eyes narrowed at the human's slip, though the knowledge did him no good.

Nicu did not have permission to pass into Witch territory. It would take far too long to attain it. He leaned his head back against the bark, felt the pain of his injury with deserved resignation.

"Why would the Queen bring the Trimarked Child here?" Nicu asked, his tongue protesting with each word, his will demanding the information.

"To trade Ember for herself," Aaron gulped, dilated eyes stuck to the tree.

Tristan's second explosion sounded without warning, this deep resonance the result of thwarted magic. The Wizard pressed against solid air, blocked from entering Witch territory.

"Oh," Aaron breathed, then his lips thinned, and he focused on Nicu. "Devi and her mom made some shield thing. I'd guess the Queen couldn't get through, if he can't."

Yet Aaron had. As a human, he had permission to travel anywhere within Trifecta that he wished. So not to draw attention, the humans would have to be allowed passage at all times, so Aaron would not be as trapped as the mages. But what could he do against the Queen, other than be caught again?

Tristan's long strides brought him to tower over Nicu and Aaron. Rage stiffened every movement.

"Make a wish," he ground out.

Power tightened. Nicu's tattoos energized. Ice filled his core. Nicu pushed to stand, ignoring the temporary black haze biting at the edges of his vision. It didn't matter that the Wizard stood a few inches taller. Nicu was wider.

"Old covenants." Nicu growled. Tristan would understand the warning where Aaron would not. Humans were not to be brought into Fate Magic. Nicu would not grant this wish.

Tristan was not impressed.

"Charlah has Ember. You are her guardian," the Wizard ground out, then lowered his bitter rage onto Aaron as the human rose from his squat. "Make a damn wish."

"Why?" Nicu demanded, his fist clenched. He blocked the direct eye contact that might lead Aaron into making a very expensive mistake. One Nicu had every intention of stopping.

"Charlah is not stable," Tristan ground out. "That alone should be enough to prove the danger. But don't forget. Ember can manipulate the Veil. The Queen has obviously been thwarted and if her family gets out—"

"It's gone," Aaron interrupted, gesturing toward himself. Tristan's rage banked, flickered into curiosity.

"How?"

Aaron swallowed and looked at his toes.

"Ember did something with a ring."

Tristan's color rose, his emerald eyes burned. "Of dragon bone?" he demanded.

"How should I know?" Aaron's irritated scowl turned thoughtful. "Wait. The Queen knew, though. Um. Yes, actually. She thought of it as The Dragon Bone ring."

Tendrils of Promise Magic pricked at Nicu's tattoos,

warmed the metal at the base of his neck, eager to be used. Nicu held strong.

"Ember took her family," Tristan spoke. "There is nothing more important to Charlah. She won't be forgiving. She'll use Ember to get out, out where you cannot stop her when she kills Ember in retaliation."

"Charlah killed a Halfer." Aaron's quiet words drifted beneath Nicu and Tristan's confrontation, and provided the manacles that clamped around Nicu's wrists.

"Make. A. Wish." Tristan stepped forward with each bitten piece of sound. He didn't spare a glance for the human who must be the one to speak. The request wouldn't matter unless Nicu agreed.

Nicu had promised to keep her safe.

His only other choice was the Trimark medallion.

He had to choose between freeing Ember's chaos, or controlling his.

Nicu turned to face Aaron.

"What's going on?" Aaron murmured. His focus flickered between each of Nicu's eyes, confusion wrinkled his forehead as he tried to understand concepts his human brain could not grasp.

"You may wish," Nicu commanded. "You will be careful with your words."

"What do I say?"

"I cannot tell you," Nicu spoke through locked teeth. "And you must be very mindful. Fae wishes are tricky things. The right one can save her."

Aaron's eyes widened, understanding that much, at least.

"I wish for Ember Lee to be rescued."

The request had been simple. Aaron had been stupid. That suited Nicu well.

Though bending physical magic eluded Nicu, he could still command the High Magic of the Fae. He'd given Ember a promise. Now he granted a wish for the hybrid girl, even if the sounds fell from a human's lips.

Dark fists clenched. The Living Ink inscribed from fingertips to torso twitched over sweat-slick skin. Tattoos flowed with the natural patterns of the world around him until they bound with the power of fate.

High Magic clung to Nicu, invaded his body. Every muscle coiled. His eyes half closed, he enforced his will.

Aaron's words hung suspended, puffs of air drifting away. Nicu grabbed them, felt the spirit inside them. He used the boy's belief, filled each syllable with purpose, spun a tale where no matter what happened with the Queen, time would adjust, space would change, all to ensure the Trimarked Child would be saved.

Wonderful, vague wish that it was, Nicu extended the power. He required it in the past. Another need stretched from the future. He held his ground, enforced his will around Aaron's words, and let the cosmos do the Work, letting the spell tie itself to the human's intent.

The energy tapered out with the balance of threes. High Magic fell into form. The universe's covenant resonated within Nicu's bones.

"What the verge is that?" Aaron grumbled, hopping back a few steps. A ribbon of light connected to his feet and moved with him, leading west into the Witch lands.

"A path," Nicu required of the Wizard. Tristan didn't hesitate as Nicu had expected, but chanted the magical tunnel into being. Nicu grasped onto Tristan's power, wove it into the trail provided by the wish.

"Go," he demanded.

Aaron ran, disappeared before Nicu's first heartbeat. Tristan tried to follow, only to be stopped solidly once again.

"I guess your magic wasn't strong enough to break that," Tristan taunted. "Are you so certain this will work?"

The Wizard's lips curled in Nicu's silence.

"That idiot child worded his wish wrong, and you know it," Tristan charged as if it were Nicu's fault. "To have her saved with no regard to her health in the process? No respect for time or place of rescue. That path he's on guarantees nothing. Charlah could still leave Trifecta with her, and the terms fulfilled by anyone else."

He stopped, eyes narrowed on Nicu.

"You must have used his vagueness to your advantage. How did you manipulate it?"

Nicu enjoyed The Wizard's tantrum. Tristan did not know the layers at work. Wish Magic was only the newest chain that bound Nicu to Ember. No matter the condition he got her back in, he would get her back. The rest could be salvaged.

Shadows slipped under Tristan's feet, slid up his legs as he shouted. The tendrils snapped into place, holding his body firm.

Branna strode to the border, leaned against the wall of energy that showed she was trapped on Witch land, though her powers weren't.

"Why do you care so much about keeping the Trimarked Child safe?" she asked the Wizard.

Tristan struggled against the inky vines long enough to realize he couldn't break them. His pointed scowl aimed toward Branna.

"She's mine."

Shadows that had nothing to do with necromancy bit at the edges of Nicu's vision. His lips pursed, then thinned, and he cursed himself for allowing his repulsion of the Wizard's words to show on his face.

"Meet me," he spoke to Branna. She nodded, agreeing to find him when able.

Nicu needed a place to rest and sort through what he'd discovered. Make a plan to gather more intel. Privacy to allow emotions to flow through his body while he was stuck not having a hand in Ember's safety, in protecting his promise to her. He would have to trust the magic to bring her back into his reach.

He would not forget today, though, nor did he discard the Wizard and his dangerous, delusional claim on the Trimarked Child. If there was one thing in this wretched Terra Nicu knew, it was that Ember Lee did not belong to that madman.

As her guardian, Nicu guaranteed it.

27

EMBER

*E*mber expected exposed roots and loose stones in the cave and tried to walk very carefully. Instead, she stumbled over the perfectly smooth, packed earth. Charlah charged forward, not needing illumination to find her way. As the tunnel continued in a straight line, and the floor remained free of debris, she trusted it as well.

Ember had to keep shaking her head to focus. Charlah's speed disoriented her. Counting her steps didn't tell her how far they traveled, but it helped her concentrate on something solid. Kept her sane. Something to do other than dwell on the Queen's secret destination.

This passage was not natural, as clean and straight as it was. Ember didn't worry about why, though she worried about what it meant for her escape route. If there was nowhere to hide, getting away would prove infinitely more difficult. Ember had her trump card, the fact that Charlah didn't like Ember's Veil energy touching her.

Once it recharged.

A glow grew as they continued deeper. Charlah might have hesitated, but Ember couldn't be sure. The grip on her wrist stiffened.

Quiet voices traveled a short distance down the tunnel. The indistinct murmurs buzzed in Ember's ears without context.

The light ahead was broken by long tendrils of hair-like growth. Charlah sneered at the offending canopy as she parted the thick curtain, leading them into a cave filled with tiny strands of seeking roots. Strange energy filtered into Ember and resonated with gentle vibration along her nerves. The space welcomed her, though Ember couldn't relax with the Queen as her guide.

Devi and Leona greeted them with deep frowns, small wisps of witchflame dashed the outer curve of the cavern. Charlah sighed and shook her head, as if the Witches were minor irritations she'd rather not deal with right now.

"What are you doing here?" Ember asked, breathless with unexpected hope. With these two, she had a genuine chance of escape.

"Pure coincidence," Devi answered, though her focus suggested they had a plan, no matter the short warning.

"Get out of the way," Charlah pouted. Mother and daughter exchanged a glance.

"You don't think there's enough room for all of us?" Leona asked. The fingers of her hands coiled into fists.

The musty air within the rounded cave stagnated. Charlah shook her head.

"Well, that wasn't very clever, barricading the tunnel," she scoffed. Charlah's free hand curled, her ragged nails resembling claws. She stepped forward. Ember planted her feet. The Queen stopped moving, the arm holding Ember fully extended. Leona placed herself between her daughter and danger.

Devi crossed her arms and cocked her hip, her brilliant green eyes flickering around the room in a way familiar to Ember. She'd seen that look many times while Devi was struggling to solve one of her complicated projects. Though Ember couldn't see Devi's puzzle, she recognized the need for time.

Ember tested the strength of her power. It was tangible,

but not strong enough to rise on its own. She wouldn't be able to rely on the energy leaking out. She might have to help it.

Ember's stomach ached, her lungs stiffened. How could she consider reaching for that power? Nicu had warned her that very morning. Intentions matter. Passive use, accidents, these were not a threat.

But choosing to reach for that power?

She thought of the hunter Fae's arrow. It would have flown if they had known Ember would act with intention.

The reviled tone in Leona's voice when Charlah had asked if the High Priestess had a hand in Ember's creation filled her mind as she stared at the woman facing the Queen. Would Leona be forgiving if Ember's use meant it saved them? Would she keep the secret?

But the real question was, could Ember truly step aside and do nothing because of what *might* happen? Would she truly put her freedom above the lives of the people around her?

Her lungs expanded on the thought, on the simple decision it brought.

She would fight. Whatever it took. The cost be damned.

"Do you have a next step?" Charlah asked Leona. "Trap the Queen, then die?"

"It's better to share a tomb with you, than let you out," Devi shrugged, a frown tugging on the corner of her mouth.

Charlah laughed.

"That's funny coming from you. You, of all people, must perceive what this place is. Sense the porous edges."

Startled, Devi looked around. Pupils expanded, darkening Devi's eyes in an echo of Charlah's. Her sharp intake of breath restored the mint color of her irises, wide and locked on the Queen.

"Now you understand why I brought her." Charlah pulled Ember forward with easy strength.

Ember's lungs threatened to seize. She squeezed quick gasps into the tight space within her chest. The blood drained from Ember's face, silently pleading with Devi to shut Charlah up before it was too late. Devi's lips thinned, eyes flickering toward the only physical weapon in their reach, though it was tucked in Charlah's belt.

Right. Focus. Fight.

The knife, then. Ember would have to reach across both their bodies to grab it. All she needed was a decent distraction.

"What does the Trimarked Child have to do with anything?" Leona asked. "If she has any magical ability, she's been bound."

"Yes, you have a senseless habit of inhibiting people. Ember. The goddess-born. It's backfired now that you don't know what those powers can do." Charlah's voice shifted into a teasing sing-song that ended in a giggle.

Leona stiffened. Devi's eyes flashed with curiosity.

"Ember is goddess-born?"

"No," Leona snapped, an answer for Devi and a warning for Charlah. Ember couldn't follow the tangled conversation, so she ignored it for more important efforts. She tugged at her wrist, slipped closer to Charlah's side as the Queen's light laugh deepened.

"This," she gasped, looking between mother and daughter. "This is worth all that time I was imprisoned. Just to be here, right now."

Leona lowered her chin, fists gripped around an unknown selection of gems. The spell she spoke vibrated through the air, the magic infused words unintelligible for Ember's human ears.

Charlah snarled at Leona. Her fingers loosened on Ember's wrist.

Ember slipped to Charlah's opposite side, eyes always on the dagger. Trembling fingers wrapped around the hilt. The Queen reacted to the contact, tossed Ember to the side. Ember winced when her bones met stone.

Charlah hadn't noticed the theft, so focused on the threat of Leona. She took a deep breath, the thin ends of her pale hair floating in the power-charged air. Nails curved into her weapon of choice.

"It took twelve Witches and Wizards to cast that spell to capture me last time," Charlah hissed. "What makes you think you can do it on your own?"

Leona didn't allow the Queen to interrupt her. Over Charlah's head, a silvery web formed. It pulsed with each shift of Leona's cadence, grew with each syllable. Devi studied the Work and added her own power and voice.

The web flared, grew from the size of a coin to the size of Ember's palm. A feral growl squeezed from Charlah and she launched herself at Leona. Her movement slowed within a few feet of the High Priestess as she hit Leona's defenses. She fought forward against the High Priestess's protective shield. Her fingers bored through the magic, aimed at Leona's mouth. Charlah gained centimeters of space as the net grew by the same.

Footsteps in the tunnel. The Witches focused on their battle of will. Ember scrambled to her feet to help mask the incoming noise and moved closer to the opening. She kept the knife low and ready.

Aaron burst into the cavern through the hanging roots. The barrier was either one way or not spelled to keep out his human body. His arm was lifted to push the curtain aside, but it also blocked his field of vision. Ember gripped his arm and pulled him back before he rushed forward into the room's chaos.

He jerked against her pull, then lost the fight when he focused on her face. He let her guide him to the rocky wall.

"How did you get here?" she hissed.

"Nicu did something," Aaron whispered back.

"He's okay?" She held her breath in hope.

"Was when I left him," Aaron agreed. Ember blinked her eyes against their sudden damp blur. Nicu was okay.

"Is he behind you?"

Aaron frowned, shook his head. "Devi and Leona barricaded the Circle. Mages can't get through."

It must be the same barrier in the cave. Ember's heart rate doubled. Nicu was alive, but not coming. Aaron added to their numbers, at least, unless Charlah infected him again.

The gossamer web twisted over Charlah's head. Ember wasn't certain how big the spell was supposed to be, but probably bigger than a dinner plate. The Queen's nails forced their way closer to Leona, who tried to step back. Charlah moved with her, offering no distance gain for the High Priestess.

Charlah glanced up at the web growing faster than she worked through Leona's shield. She abandoned her fight and turned to Ember, gripping her by the shoulders. Aaron grabbed Ember's wrist.

"You are not welcome!" Charlah hissed to Aaron, shoving him while jerking Ember forward. Ember loosened her grip on the knife, left it in Aaron's grasping hand.

"She won't stop her spell. You need to open the door. Get us out of here," Charlah ordered.

"I don't know how," Ember argued, glancing at the web. It had grown only a few centimeters. Though it followed the Queen, it couldn't keep up with her changes of direction. It was too slow, in growth and pace.

The truth did not satisfy the Queen. She scratched the roots away from the rocky wall, then grabbed Ember's wrist and forced her palm against the surface.

Movement caught her peripheral attention. Charlah's arm lashed out, stopping Aaron's starfall blade attack. He flew to the left, the knife clattering in the opposite direction. Charlah put pressure on Ember's fingers so her skin indented with each hard, sharp variation of the stone.

"Figure it out," the Queen demanded. "You won't like the other way."

Leona's voice filled the cave with grounded confidence. Devi matched it with her own insistent power. And the web grew another inch. Could she get Charlah closer to it? Or maybe buy time?

"Okay." Ember declared. "I will try."

Ember leaned her weight into the wall, focused deep within her, found the barest puddling of energy at the base of her spine and grit her teeth. She fed the fear tightening her chest, pulled images of afflicted Halfers, remembered the overbearing fog in her mother's mind. Sparks snapped along her spine, lots of them, rising fast.

Use without control. Ember fed the power. Let go of the discipline she'd honed while living with the Halfers, and let the energy surge.

Charlah's growled shriek blasted Ember's ear even as the echo of blue light filtered through Ember's closed lids. Then, Ember's hand was free. She opened her eyes to see dying sparks, the space where the Queen had been was empty. She spun her back toward the wall to see Charlah had appeared next to the starfall dagger.

Ember looked to Aaron, who had regained his feet, but stared at the ground with a deeply furrowed brow. She dismissed him when Charlah returned to her attack on Leona's shield, this time using the knife to hack through the thickened air.

Ember's eyes widened, remembered that this knife was the one to cut through the barrier. Could it cut through the Witch's shield?

"Leona!" Aaron cried, apparently having the same thought. But instead of rushing toward her, he looked back to the ground. His foot brushed against the dirt floor. He used the force meant for sending a soccer ball flying across the pitch. A small, dark object flew through the cave, aimed for the High Priestess.

"No!" Charlah and Leona called as one, in odd agreement. Charlah grabbed Leona from behind and wrapped her free arm under the priestess's chin and pressed her jaw closed.

Leona struggled to keep up her chant. The knife inched toward her neck, slowly cutting through her protective spell.

The ring shifted direction on its own. Devi lifted her arms as if to ward it off. The circlet slid onto the middle finger of her right hand like it belonged there.

Leona choked on starfall iron. Fresh air filled the tunnel, the shield against the entrance gone. Charlah's fingers splattered in blood as she yanked the blade free, a stab meant to stop the Witch from making another sound, directing any magic.

The High Priestess fell.

A blue glow surrounded Ember in an explosion of self-preservation.

Devi's rage dwarfed Ember's glow. Blind with emotion, she pulled at whatever magic she found. The energies of the cave rushed to her command. She reached into Ember's DNA to drag particles of blue energy from her veins, unaware of the source, willing to use it all against the Queen.

Ember's breath caught. Her ears filled with a high pitched whir. She gripped her ribs against the need to vomit as she felt the energy rip through her pores, claimed by someone it did not belong to.

Tristan had said something about this. Her power needed to be given, not taken. Then it wouldn't hurt.

So Ember let go. She gave it with empathy to the Witch who had watched her mother die. Offered it in guilt, as an undercurrent of relief sighed within Ember, whispered that she was safe from exposure by the High Priestess of Trifecta's Circle.

Devi let loose a cyclone of her power and Ember's, a tangled twist of transparent magic and blue-tinted Veil energy. The web that had fallen with Leona sprung back into existence, now the size of a small blanket. Devi angled it so it blocked Charlah from the exit. Charlah produced an angry, guttural gasp and shot to the opposite side of the cave.

The net couldn't move from the entrance. It needed to be bigger. Devi Worked furiously, her voice a throat-ripping growl, her focus violent.

Ember closed her eyes, tried to offer more of her power to the cause. It trickled from her. A tap turned on low.

Blood intensifies magic.

They needed a storm.

Ember bit her lip until she tasted copper.

The web burst with light, as large as the cavern itself, and closed in on the Queen. The knife flashed, caught on the web of power, stretched and deformed the magic until it ripped through the middle, providing a path for Charlah to escape.

"Sh-should we go after her?" Aaron asked, his feet frozen in place. Ember wanted to collapse, not chase the Queen.

"I will find her," Devi declared, though her shoulders wilted, her eyes locked onto Leona's form. Blood seeped into the floor.

The roots twitched as if in the tunnel's breeze, then bent in concert. Tendrils stretched, grew along the ground, hunting the High Priestess.

"Is this cave under No Man's?" he demanded.

"Yes." Devi answered, even as she rebuilt the web meant for Charlah, changing its purpose to gather the tree's tentacles and pin them against the edges of the cavern. The thicker roots wiggled in captivity. Thinner threads worked between the weave of magic, wrapped around the spell until it snapped with the pressure.

"They must be from the tree growing there now - don't let them touch her!" Aaron shouted, kicking and hitting at the plant growth as he rushed toward Leona's body. "We have to get her out of here. This tree ate Brandt."

Ember didn't ask how he knew, just trusted the rough truth in his voice. Devi bared her teeth, struggling to hold the frayed magic in form, out of time to restart. She was losing the battle.

Ember looked between the human and the Witch, both fighting to protect the fallen.

Terror shook her, but she knew what she had to do.

She had to engage her power. Purposefully.

The shield was already on her skin. She just had to manipulate it.

"Carry her," Ember ordered. Aaron flinched, but wrapped his arms around Leona's body, tender as he lifted her. Devi backed up to them, holding the spell. Two tears dripped to her cheeks.

Ember wasn't drained like she'd been with the ring, or after creating the storm. Perhaps giving her power to Devi had not only stopped the pain, but allowed her to keep some in reserve.

She placed her palm on Aaron's back and forced the blue energy from her skin. Convinced Aaron wouldn't hurt her, she compelled herself into feeling secure. His warmth radiated through his coat. The shield eased from Ember, spread across Aaron, and from him to Leona. Ember wrapped her other hand around Devi's bicep and power coated the Witch. Ember didn't stop until every inch of them was within its shell.

The roots froze, then drifted back into place, unable to sense their prey. Devi stopped her chant, her chest heaving. The webbing fell apart in specks of power. The Witch's trembling hand covered Ember's fingers where they held her.

Then Ember pulled them all out.

28

EMBER

They walked into the Circle with slow steps, the sky red with the setting sun. Ember had lost her hold on the shield just before they stepped out of the cave. Her use of this odd power caught up to her, leaving her drained.

A heavy lump filled her stomach. Tears pricked her eyes. She'd crossed a line by using her power. Losing the High Priestess weighed on her heart, as well, though guilty relief softened her grief.

Leona was gone. Whether she'd discovered Ember's secret or not was no longer a concern.

Ember had to live with the consequences of her choices, for wielding the Veil energy purposefully. For protecting her friends.

She shivered at the thought, wrapped her elbows with chilled fingers. The adrenaline had worn off and cold bit her from the outside.

The Witches and Wizards of Trifecta met them with silence. As they realized who Aaron carried, the sorrow on their faces shifted. They hadn't processed their time while afflicted, and now they found their High Priestess dead in the arms of the human boy who brought her home.

Eventually, one Wizard came forward and took Leona from Aaron's arms. He transferred her with a forlorn nod, the trembling in his arms apparent as her weight was taken from them. He'd struggled, but he'd never said a word, never suggested a pause.

Devi watched the Wizard for a moment, playing with the ring newly placed on her finger. Clenching her fist around it, she turned on her heel. Her hair fell from a ripped apart bun as she followed the body of her mom.

Aaron and Ember were not invited, would not have asked. They walked in silence until they reached the fountain in the entry gardens. Ember remembered Aaron had watched its creation with amazement five weeks ago. Now Chase and Susan waited on a bench at its edge. Susan stared at her clenched hands, as if she were afraid to touch anything in case it would infect her with magic.

"Mom," Ember called, her voice breaking. Susan whipped around, her eyes wide. Giant tears dropped from thin lower lashes, and she fumbled her way into a hug with Ember. A vision of Susan being in Leona's place wrenched at Ember's heart. She returned the desperation of her mother's embrace, grateful for this break in Susan's animosity. Gratified she was present in the exact moment Ember needed it.

"What the verge did you do?" Chase growled. Ember released the pressure on her eyelids to find him pawing at Aaron. The Halfer checked out Aaron's neck, then forcefully tried to open the blood soaked coat that had seized his attention. He ignored Aaron's attempts to stop him and Aaron had to try a few times before he caught Chase's smaller wrists. With a dip of his knees, Aaron pulled the Halfer's eyes to his own.

"It isn't mine," he promised, his voice tired, broken. Aaron hesitated. He stepped closer to Chase, keeping a hold of his hands. "Chase, I'm so sorry."

And Ember remembered. Tears spilled over her cheeks, not

wanting Aaron to say the words. Not wanting Chase to hear them.

"Leona didn't make it. Charlah kill—your mom didn't make it."

Susan slipped from her hug to stare wide eyed, fingers trembling against her lips with the news.

"Oh," Chase whispered, his fingers flexing in Aaron's grasp. "Oh. I." He cleared his throat and moved their linked hands forward, re-zipping Aaron's coat. "I'm glad you're okay."

Chase's eyes glazed, and his Adam's apple bobbed when he swallowed.

"Why don't you go find Devi?" Aaron suggested.

"She won't let me see coven stuff," Chase argued, his voice hollow and rough.

"She will today," Ember assured him, clearing her face with the cuffs of her coat.

"I have to get you back," he tried again. Aaron tugged Chase into a hug, then set him on course to head deeper into the Circle.

"I'll take them. Go be with—" Aaron frowned. "Just go."

Chase walked away without further acknowledgement. He drifted into the group of Witches and Wizards leaving their apartments on their way to honor their High Priestess.

Susan grasped through the air, her fingers searching until she held Ember's hand. Ember took it without comment, not wanting to break whatever spell that had her mother choosing to be at her side.

Ember's lips lifted in a humorless curve. This was her first ever positive thought that included both her mom and magic.

"Ready?" Aaron asked. She shrugged, the answer an obvious no. They had to go, anyway. Ember eyed him as they left the Circle.

"What are you going to tell your dad about all that blood?" she asked. Aaron looked at himself with a grimace, then a shrug.

"Hope to sneak in without him seeing?" He didn't sound hopeful.

"We could stop at Chase's house," she offered hesitantly. "You can clean up. Borrow something. He won't mind."

"Good idea," Aaron agreed after a moment. "Should we take your mom home, first?"

Susan's hand squeezed Ember's fingers until their bones collided. Ember winced at the pain, thought of the night before, when Chase had walked her to Susan's. She hadn't been able to go inside to check on her mom then. She wasn't ready to say goodbye now.

"I think it will be fine. It's on the way," Ember said.

Their feet crossed from gravel to broken concrete. The street was deserted, the Halfers hiding underground until their leader returned. Ember rolled her shoulders, thankful for not having to encounter them right now.

"Um, thanks for the shielding," Aaron murmured. Ember's lips flickered up in response.

"Least I could do, since you came charging in to rescue us."

"You," Aaron blurted, then looked at the toes of his shoes. "I mean, of course."

They reached Chase's house, but instead of going straight in, they stopped in the center of the road. Ember wondered where Charlah was, if she was stalking them at this moment. She took a deep breath and studied the shadows, opening her mind to the twilight.

The breeze brought with it a pocket of warmth, the scent of pine and mist, and the last coils of tension sank through her feet.

Nicu was out there. Charlah wouldn't be bothering them. She wouldn't have figured out what to do with them, anyway, now that they were working together.

"It was nice, being a team," Aaron echoed Ember's thoughts, staring at the stars. He turned the sparkle in his blue eyes on to her, attacked her with his crooked, puppy dog smirk. "Like friends."

Ember's smile grew, her lips soft in its curve. She wrapped an arm around her mom, who had begun to shiver, and moved toward the smallest house on the block.

"Yeah, it was," she spoke over her shoulder, not looking back to see the goofy grin she knew he'd be wearing.

29

NICU

"She is walking a bit stiffly," Branna murmured as they watched the small group from the trees. Aaron opened the door, then waved the women in before following behind.

Nicu ignored Branna, grateful Ember wasn't badly wounded. Thankful the blood soaked Aaron, not her. Though, the human's easy movements suggested it wasn't his.

"We need to discover what happened," he said.

Though he'd monitored the High Magic surrounding the Trimarked Child, he'd only gained assurance she was alive. Until he could learn what occurred while she'd been out of sight, he must practice patience.

"And we will." Branna's voice was sharp, determined. "But for now, let us speak of today's irregularities."

Nicu noted the skin drawn tight over Branna's cheekbones, the thin line of her lips. Shadows darkened around them, thanks to the setting sun. They needed more privacy if they were to enter into this conversation. He thinned his lips to pantomime silence, his sight in line with the darkest shadows. Branna glared, but did as he couldn't ask, and cloaked them.

"All anomalies?" he asked quietly, glancing toward her

hands where tattoos curved onto her palms. Branna snapped her fists closed, then nodded as she glanced away.

Satisfied, she would share, Nicu raised steady hands and removed the winter-gray talisman from under his braids. He held it suspended by a fine cord of hemp. Branna glanced at the spinning piece in dismissal.

Drew in a sharp breath when she processed what she'd seen.

"Nicu, what did you do? How long have you carried that?"

"Five weeks," he admitted. "The pain you felt."

Branna gasped. Her hands gripped each other in front of her heart. They both recalled the moment Branna cried out through the forest. A searing spasm ripped through her as Nicu's slightest brush against the medallion frayed the magical bond the Fae had placed between them.

"I saw Brandt about to strike Ember. My purpose... Branna, had I known you would respond to its use —"

"Enough." Branna focused on her breath. Both Fae studied the spinning pentacle with folded wings. Latched securely on one side, the lacy metal was decorated with delicate chains and patterned links. Unclasping the butterfly had saved Ember from the knife, but trapped her in the barrier. The simple flicker had sent Branna to her knees.

There was no telling what might have happened if he opened it fully.

Yet, there was more to confess.

"It started as an option. It has become a temptation. I almost used it today even knowing it would cause you pain."

"What stopped you?"

"You do not want to know."

Thoughts flickered in the ticks and shifts of Branna's face. As he waited, Nicu meditated on the slow spin of the metal dangling from his hand, it's power bound by a simple clasp. A beautiful piece of jewelry with a treacherous purpose.

"Perhaps, those five weeks ago, I would have found

another solution, had this one been unavailable. I used the Trimark in haste. I might do so again." Nicu extended his hand. Branna recoiled. "This connects to you as well. You should hold it. Decide if the moment calls."

Trust offered. Wist's possible truth withheld. The story of granting a wish, a matter of omission. High Magic that gifted him one more occasion to resist the temptation of the talisman.

Branna extended a single finger toward the butterfly wing. The mark echoed the tattoo of Binding Ink locked onto the back of the Trimarked Child's neck, though her pentacle was slashed while the medallion remained free. Her magic contained. And this was the key.

Branna withdrew.

"Just because I can speak to the dead does not make me unexpectedly wise." She spoke with a centeredness Nicu was unused to from this dark and fiery Fae. She met his amber eyes, the lightest shade of all the Fae, bleached at the hybrid girl's birth.

"I do know you, though, Nicu Coccia. I have found you to be as torn between worlds as I am. It is wise to collect options. And ..." Branna inhaled deeply through her nose. She opened her hands and withdrew her tattoos to show how the creases in her skin had taken on a grey tint, as if someone had drawn them on with chalk.

"Whatever you did, opened up my powers," she whispered, even deep in the shadows.

"I hurt you. I will hurt you again if I use it." His words were quiet, his lips firm with certainty. She must understand the risk. He needed her to emote, to tip the scale. A calm Branna was not the one he wanted at this moment.

"Yes." Her answer was simple. Direct. "But whatever this change in my skin is, it does not hurt. And the access to the shadows ..."

Branna closed her eyes and drew the darkness in, bathing them in her power.

"I would not have this taken away. It feels like coming home."

He froze. "You would have me open the Trimark, then?"

Branna snorted, returned to her semi-controlled self, easing the shadows so they still had privacy, but could clearly see one another.

"I will not tell you what to do. You wouldn't listen to me, anyway, when the time came." She eased her posture away from him, provided space. "I won't offer myself as a sacrifice. I know better than to get between you and the Trimarked Child. You will only have yourself to blame, whatever your choice."

Nicu flinched at the truth.

He thought he had dodged this double-edged sword ten years ago, turned it into a balance rope with a promise given. He glared at the Trimark, then swept it up under the fall of his braids, tucked against his spine.

"Edan made a deal with the Trimarked Child. He wanted to check with his scouts on the outside. I have not spoken to him for almost as long as you. I do not have your answers." A gift from him for her honesty.

Branna's eyes widened with the information, a very quiet reaction from the usually volatile Fae that spoke of the depth of her hurt.

Nicu turned his attention back to the Halfer zone to allow her the space she needed, and returned his thoughts toward the Trimarked Child. Branna's words were correct, of course.

He'd intended to gratify his dual loyalties when he'd stolen the talisman from the vaults. Instead, he found it forcing a decision he wasn't willing to make. Yet.

Today, he realized he had more things to learn about the Gypsum Fae. To discover what promises they kept, which were broken, and those that were false.

Before he lost his balance and had to choose on which side to fall.

EPILOGUE

TRISTAN

The lurid afternoon faded into a russet evening. A single tree in the dead clearing allowed more of the autumnal sunlight to streak through its branches as the rest of the forest settled in for an early night.

The Witch fence had flickered out, evident by Branna's stumbling step into No Man's as she'd been leaning against it. She'd withdrawn her shadows and disappeared before he could turn around, likely moving in the shadows. An enviable talent, though he didn't care for the side effects. The marks of ashy skin on her palms was the beginning of a condition he'd seen once before.

While on the outside, a Fae who took any work for the right fee procured him the pinecone seed for this special tree. That Fae, Cyrene, had faded quickly, her entire surface marbled grey between one meeting and the next. The results interesting, but not pretty.

"You're making a mistake, Tristan."

Charlah stood beside him, mimicking his study of the giant sequoia. When she turned her storm cloud irises on to him, he glanced at her belt. Charlah's yellow and black gems had morphed into pewter spheres, similar to small ball bullets. One of his sister's other personalities had risen.

"Ah. Lyla," he acknowledged the alternate personality.

This would make things more difficult.

"I understand why you woke Charlah instead of me. How it might make this easier. But really, how did you expect to control her?" Her pale brow rose. Tristan's frown fell sharp at the reprimand in his elder sister's voice.

"I expected her to remain groggy for a while longer."

Bell-tone laugher struck the trees that surrounded, the sound dying within the expanse of No Man's.

"Your miscalculations should be legendary."

"They're hardly nuisances," Tristan ground out. With a sigh, he released the tension brought on by his sister's teasing, almost like they were a real family. "Now what?" he asked.

"Now, I will give you what you want." Tristan bent in a bow of thanks. Lyla's sharp glance stopped him. "Only part of it. I repeat. You are making a mistake. Yet, you've already started, and what is a big sister to do except support her little brother?"

"It isn't like this is a scrape I need help out of." His throat tightened around the words, his eyes narrowed against her judgement.

"Really? Then why did you release that Fae when you need their soul touch, too?"

Tristan's eyes narrowed. "Proof you don't know everything."

"I know enough to help you without getting myself killed," Lyla countered.

His sister reached for the woven hemp chain around her neck and pulled the large crystal from her chest. With reverent fingers, she slipped the gem from its gentle cage, holding on to the length of the rope.

"Whether it be your triumph or your failure, Tristan, this is on you. But I will make you work for it, either way."

Lyla released the crystal, and it floated between her curved hands. She brought the tips of her fingers together and twisted in opposite directions. The crystal split into three portions, two domes and one flattened cylinder.

"Stop!" Tristan grabbed for the gem only to find the space manipulated. His arm reached forward at full length, yet came no closer to his stationary sister.

He retracted his fist and clenched his jaw.

"What is this?" he demanded.

"Survival."

"This will not get us back to Heldu!"

"Why, brother dear, would you assume I was speaking about your survival?"

The hemp wrapped around the right domed piece of crystal, then floated back around her neck. She turned to face Tristan. The remaining pieces of crystal rested in her palms, a clear-as-glass dome and a deep, milky cylinder that had been the center.

"You will want to keep the domed portion for yourself," she informed him. "The third piece will grow your tree."

Tristan's gaze left Lyla's to take in the gift she presented him.

"You're right," he agreed grudgingly. "I should have awoken you, first."

Lyla snorted. "If Charlah hadn't caused all this havoc, if she hadn't shown me the limitations of this bubble... Well. I would have been less helpful."

Tristan reached. He gained ground, but still could not connect with his prize. He met Lyla's human-like eyes.

"You have been very lucky, little brother," Lyla warned. "For now, that boy and I have paid the price. You will not continue to be so fortunate. You better succeed, or the cost will not justify your means. Fate is rarely kind."

"It will work," Tristan assured her. "We will get back to Heldu. The Fae will pay for their manipulations."

Lyla studied Tristan for a long moment. She breathed deeply, and Tristan felt her magic ease, allowing him to take possession of the last two pieces of soul crystal.

The second the cool gems rested in his palm, the light left Lyla's eyes. Charlah bounced back in for only a moment, but even she faded. The universes solidified lash to lash, hardening into tarnished pewter. The stones on her belt shifted until each one was a different shade and clarity of quartz.

This was a personality Tristan had not met. The shock and recognition in the shape of her mouth suggested she knew him. With a gasp, the woman wrapped magic around her and disappeared.

No path. No break in the Veil.

Yet, gone.

Tristan smiled. He wouldn't attempt to find the portion of his sister's soul who ran away. He had what he wanted, and if anything was certain, that creature could take care of herself.

He'd based his experiment on Ember on what he'd learned from his parent's attempts with his elder sibling. Trying to make a goddess was hard, impossible work. The beings that resulted, however, were always amazing.

And Lyla's gift would help Tristan with his task. His sister's role was complete. Ember's was yet to come.

ACKNOWLEDGMENTS

This last year has not been easy for any of us. I hope Ember's story can bring some mental relief. We are all, in a way, trapped by circumstances. Yet, we make the best of them. We fight for our physical health, mental health, and to have healthy relationships. We are all Ember, Nicu, Devi, Aaron, Branna, and Chase.

So, this story's acknowledgments are for you. For all of us. For the hard work we've put into forging new paths and discovering new ways to have friendships. Finding reminders that we are all very similar, that we all struggle, and that we can all do our best with whatever afflictions we face.

Congratulations on your wins.
C.K. Sorens

ABOUT THE AUTHOR

C.K. Sorens, a USA Today Bestselling author of Defiant Fantasy, writes dark fantasy and romantasy that explore fate, choice, and resilience. Known for her character-driven stories and compelling worlds, Sorens' works include the urban fantasy Trimarked series and the romantasy *Eighteen Wishes*. When not writing, she enjoys hiking, puzzles, and family adventures.

Discover more about C.K. Sorens' worlds of Defiant Fantasy and explore her latest releases at <u>www.cksorens.com</u>.

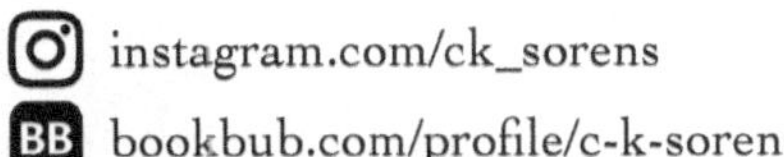 instagram.com/ck_sorens

bookbub.com/profile/c-k-sorens